THE COVERLY HILLS

I AM YOUR KILLER

KALIMISETTY ANANDBABU

ISBN:9798581413548

Cover design by: Art Painter
Library of Congress Control Number: 2018675309
Printed in the United States of America

I dedicate this book to my beloved father Late sri K.Munayya, My mother K.Lakshmidevi,My wife K.Padam-avathi,My daughter K.Alekhya and My son K.Munikran

"Life is not for misery,It is for joy and Happiness".
Swami Vivekananda

CONTENTS

PREFACE

My passion in my life is to become a great author in all zoners.Particularly I love writing the most thrillng suspense novels with crime.I would like to make my audience thrilled every minute while reading my book.I hope this book'The coverly Hills" Gives pleasure to the reader having thrilling suspense at every moment.

I would like to thank My Brother K.Ramesh Babu who has supported me in writing this book; I am also thankful to my colleagues P.Janardhan Reddy , K.Nagaraju , M.Vijaya bhaskar reddy,K.Nageswar reddy Who always inspired me to continue my writing.Finally,I would like to thank all my Well wishers who have hleped me in this project..

PROLOGUE

London shivered hearing about serial killings...The amateur psycho killer successfully killed Three people,A police officer,A couple at the beach,..the psychoKiller next target is The Train expedition of 'coverly hills'...

Detective Roberts Entered the scene.He Chased the killer..They both travelled in the same train..But The killer successfully killed one by one on the journey.At every stay,There is chasing,tension and mysterious murders.The killer focus is on compartment number.2,The killer targetted couples mostly.Roberts tried to stop the killings and catch the killer, But In vain. 'I am your killer' is the tag for the killer

Who is the serial killer?

Why the killer is doing all this?...

Read and learn about it..

CHAPTER I

THE THRILLING EXPERIENCE

L ondon...
Broadway...
Night 10 PM...

"Wind Castle Theatre", A play is going on "As I know how to kill". The audience are in thrilling moment. Actors are very busy.

"I don't want to kill you Julia ... But you have made it compulsion. I don't want to lose my temper... But your behavior made me to act... I am ready to kill you ... come on ... sacrifice your life for me ... you are mine ... mine only ... I don't allow others enter in your life".

The words of the actor made audience come to the edge of their seats. Julia terrified "No ... Grisham ... No ...", she is pleading "Don't kill me ... I am your lover".

"Lover of me ... or my money ...", He neared to her.

All the audience are at the edge of their seats. He took out a knife. It is sparkling in the light.

"I wanna kill you ... I wanna kill you', rhymingly he is saying. She frightenly says, "No", He attacked her with the knife and stabbed her. Blood is running.

A sudden cry of joy and loud words made audience stunned. A man in blue coat stood there and hysterically saying.

"Kill her ... kill her ... oh my goodness! ... kill her ... don't leave her". He was clapping his hands. The strange looks of audience didn't disturb him. The scene completed, he came out of the theatre. It was a chilly day. There was a small drizzle. The man in blue coat adjusted his muffler around his neck. He wore gloves taking from his pocket and started moving to the centre. Keeping his hands in his pocket, he was murmuring.

'Ya ... that's right ... killing her is right. Wow! What a scene", exclaiming that he was walking on the road.

There were a few pedestrians on the road. Some cars are moving from north to south.

Night 11 PM, all the shops were closed. The small drizzle gives pain to the pedestrians. There were only a few on the road. A police man was moving door to door checking the Avenue.

"Excuse me ...", the police man turned his head. The man in blue coat with muffler around his neck stood before him.

"I am Mr. John from America".

"Yes, what can I do for you Gentleman?"

"I would like to go to Danton's street ... But no taxi I couldn't find".

"Now, it is very difficult to go there. You can't find taxi".

"Why?"

"You don't know, this is not the right time to go there".

"Hmm...",

"No taxi person is willing come with you", The police personnel said.

"O.K. sir ... How far is it?".

"It's 5 miles from here".

"O.K. Thank you officer", greeting him the man in coat walked away into a dark lane. The police officer looked at him in a strange manner. He resumed his journey trying the doors.

"Bang", there was suddenly a blow on the head of the police officer. A heavy rod touched the back of the head.

"Oh ... my ...", he wanted to turn back but again another blow ... He looked at with blurred eyes covering with blood, the man in long coat. He dragged the police man into a dark lane. He was humming "I wanna kill you ... I wanna kill you".

"Why", the police officer questioned. There is no reply. The man shifted the rod to the left hand. Without waiting, he attacked.

"Bang … Bang … Bang", there was a blood shed.

"Ya … The first attempt is successful", saying this, he slipped into the darkness.

Police head quarters, London.

Morning 10 o'clock.

There was a drizzling outside. Roberts, detective entered the office. He was in black suit, aged 60. His brown eyes give him different look. Everyone was greeting him. He came to the chief chamber directly. The receptionist greeted him. He asked," Where is the boss?"

"In his chamber sir", she replied, "Waiting for you". He entered the chamber knocking the door.

"Come in Gentleman … Have a seat",

"Thank you sir", he seated.

"Last night a police officer, Mr. Morgan has been murdered brutally".

"I heard about it, sir".

"Mr. Mathews was handling the case. The murder happened night 11 PM. We got the information this morning".

"Yes sir ... It is an unfortunate incident".

"I need your help Roberts ... In my experience, I am telling you that it is the act of a 'psycho killer'.

"Ya sir ... you are right ... The killer used his rod repeatedly, may be 'A psycho' can kill like that brutally.

"Sir ... can we go to the scene of offence?"

"Sure", saying that he came out of his chamber. Roberts followed him. The office was alert. Everyone was discussing about the murder. All became silent watching the chief coming out. It was raining Roberts sat with the chief in his car. The car was moving on followed by two security cars.

"The police officer doesn't have any controversies with any one",

"Yes sir ... this morning I checked his past history ... he doesn't have any controversies and connections with criminals", He replied.

"Psychos don't want reasons to kill ... They get pleasure from it", The chief said.

The cars were running fast to the death spot.

The cars reached the broad way centre. They came out of the car and moved to a small lane where the scene of offence occurred. The area is blocked by the police. Because of heavy rain, all the blood marks were removed.

Mathews, the in charge of the case, saluted the chief. "Any progress?", the chief asked him.

"Yes sir, we shifted the dead body to the hospital. Finger print experts tried to find the killer's finger prints. But, it is unfortunate that because of heavy rain, they didn't find any finger prints. Dog squad came here but dogs went upto the centre and didn't give any clue about murderer sir".

Listening to that, the chief sighed, Roberts eyes were searching the place and he moved to the spot to find the clue. He walked a few yards in the lane. There was nothing strange. But he stopped at a place. There is a newspaper with a blood stain. It is wet. He bent and took it carefully. Taking it, he kept it in a plastic cover carefully. He inspected the place, but he didn't find any other clue.

"Sir, with your kind permission, I go to the mortuary of the hospital. I want to examine the dead body of the police officer".

"Surely Roberts … Is there any clue?",

"Yes sir, after examining the body, I will discuss with you".

"Ok … fine then". Saying that , the chief left the place. Roberts stood there and lit his cigar.

"What do you say about this case Roberts?", Mathews asked him.

Roberts smiled, but didn't give any reply to Mathews.

"Firstly I have to examine the dead body … then I can get conclusion", saying that Roberts called a taxi.

"May I come in, sir!", Roberts asked the chief.

"You already came to my room Roberts", the chief laughed at him. Roberts with a smile sat before him." Tell me Roberts about the progress".

"No doubt sir, It is done by a psycho, but not experienced. He is a young psycho. May be it is his first murder".

"How do you know?", The chief knotted his fore head.

"Sir, An experienced psycho does his work with perfection. I examined the body of our police officer. The psycho attacked him with a rod and repeatedly he blew his head. An experienced psycho doesn't attack like that ... May be he is an amateur killer."

Chief asked him, "Any clue?"

"Yes sir ...", he took out the newspaper from his pocket. He opened it and showed him a news item to it. Still there is a blood stain at the corner of the news paper.

Chief asked him, "What is it?"

"Sir, Read the advertisement", Roberts asked.

The chief took it and observed the date of the paper.It is the paper of one week back.He observed blood stains on the paper.

He opened it and started reading.It is very interesting news.

Come and Join!

Coverly Hills Adventurous Expedition

(Manchester Club Organisation)

Do you want to do adventurous journey in your life!

Here is a great opportunity !!!

Explore dangerous hills, thickly dense forest, caves, haunted houses, water falls ... many more...

Adventurous thrilling and joyful ride by train with great arrangements

Once in a life time chance ... Hurry!

Last hours to book your ticket.

Caution: journey should be at your own risk. Management shouldn't take responsibility of expediters.

Contact: Secretary,

Manchester Club Organisation

Down town Street,

London

Contact No: +011224657

Mail: mco1569@gmail.com

"What is the connection to this advertisement with

the case".The chief asked.

"Sir, may be the psycho killer is making this journey".

"How can you say?", the chief asked.

"Psychos create opportunities to catch its prey alone … They like to choose the lonely places to make their adventures. The blood stain shows the killer had the news paper with him … that to this advertisement. So, I surely believe that he has chosen the expedition is one of his greatest opportunities".

"Hmm…", The chief sighed -------

"Shall we warn the authorities about it?"

"No sir, there is no use of it. They don't believe our guessing", Roberts replied.

"What should we do?", the chief questioned.

"I travel as a passenger in the train".

"Ok … I shall arrange tickets for the trip".

"O.K sir … I am leaving now", saying this, Roberts left the room of the chief.

The chief opened the news paper and found in a corner some words written with the blood of police officer.

"I AM YOUR KILLER".

CHAPTER II

MURDER ON BEACH

Fistral Beach...
Time 6 PM...

One of the finest beaches in England ... It is famous for surfing. It feels secluded and peaceful. The beach is a few miles away from popular seaside town, Newquay. It is blessed with soft sand and rugged hills. Most of the surfers like to surf here, because the waves are strong at times. A collection of restaurants and bars attract somany visitors at the weekend.

Gary and Maria were lying on the soft sand. The cool breeze touches their body giving pleasure to them. Gary smiled.

"How beautiful the weather is!", He commented.

Maria didn't give reply. She watched the surroundings. It is not the weekend. There are only a few people on the beach. They both are engaged. Gary asked her so many times to come with him outing, she agreed to it finally.

Gary didn't want to lose his chance … He neared to her, his hot breath is touching her ears. He whispered, "I want you now". Her cheeks blushed in red. He cluched her in his hands. Her blood is running like waves suddenly. It was drizzling. The rain drops falling on her body were running smoothly. He kissed on her lips. Rain became very heavy. The heavy clouds are covering the Sun, which have made the total area dark. The sounds of the visitors of the beach could here, but they didn't care for it.

"How beautiful you are!", The husky voice of Roberts made her close her eyes with shy.

Suddenly there was a sound of foot steps. Gary firstly aware of it. He saw someone in raincoat coming to them. The rain was pouring. There was the music of beatles coming out from the radio.

"Who are you man?" Gary asked him.

The man didn't give any reply. The radio which is in his coat plays the music.

'Hey, what do you want?" Gary asked him leaving Maria. Maria was looking at him strangely. The man wore a blue rounded hat wearing a mask to his mouth.

"I wanna kill you", The man replied cooly.

Gary Shivered, 'What!",

Before saying this, the man in blue coat took out a rod and banged on the head of Gary. "BANG", the sound of the rod frightened Maria. Gary fell down, the blood was bleeding on his head. Maria cried in horror. But her loud cries subsided in the heavy rain. She tried to run. The killer threw the rod on her legs. She fell down. He came nearer to her.

"Don't kill me", she pleaded. He laughed at, "O.K. I will leave you … but if I leave you … You won't tell the information about me others. Promise me".

"Promise!" fearfully she says.

"How can you promise me like that ! He is your lover! Your life! but you cheated him making a promise to me", saying that he took out a knife.

"I wanna kill you! I wanna kill you!", saying that he cut her throat. She tried to cry, but it was of no use! The blood was bleeding from her throat. The music of beatles was coming faintly. The killer sat by her. He was enjoying the music. The rain was continuously pouring.

"Wow, how beautiful the day is!", he was thinking of joy.

The dead bodies of the couple were spread aside. The killer opened a dark chocolate and started eating. The lighting of the light house is faintly falling on the beach. The rain became very heavy.

6 A.M.

Roberts house,

The phone rang wildly. Roberts opened his eyes. He lifted the phone.

"Where are you Roberts?", the chief asked. "At home sir", he replied.

"Can you come to Fistral beach?"

"Sure sir. I will be there," saying that he got out of the bed and went to the mirror. His white hair shows his experience. Watching his face on the mirror, he sighed. He has been in the profession nearly for 30 years. He is a dedicated police officer with no rewards. He is a very sincere officer with much respect in the department.

"Hurry up man!", saying to himself, he went into the bathroom.

When he reached the beach, there were so many people interestingly watching the scene. The police officers covered the area with protection. Roberts came out of the car. Early morning environment on the beach was pleasant. He lit his cigar watching the gathered crowd.

"Hi Roberts!", Sandy greeted him.

"Hi", he replied.

"Again brutal murder of couple by the killer".

He went near by the spot. He saw the dead bodies of the couple.

"The same killer, The same weapon," He sighed.

There was a police car siren, the chief arrived.

"Roberts," called the chief.

"Sir".

"Again it happened", the chief asked him.

"Yes sir, the same killer".

"how can you say?"

"The same blow on the head of the man using rod".

"Hmm", the chief sighed.

"Can't we catch the killer early?"

"Yes sir, surely I should try", saying that he found a chocolate wrapper near by the dead bodies of the couple. He took it.

The chief looked at it and said "How strange! After killing someone, staying there and eating chocolate".

"Nothing strange sir! Psychos get pleasure doing like that".

"How do you know that?" The chief asked him.

"Sir, I did specialization in 'psycho criminology' Roberts said, "According to it, the killer is doing all these murders purely for his pleasure only. Generally this kind of people doesn't do killing purposely. They kill the others for their pleasure and fame. All the people have to talk about their deeds. They listen and satisfy".

"Hmm", The chief sighed, "Roberts, it is your responsibility to catch the killer. You should solve it as early as possible".

"You know sir … I have booked my tickets to 'Coverly Hills Expedition'. The journey begins next Sunday … I guess the killer travels with it".

"I have already told you that I will make necessary arrangements".

"Sir, I wish to travel secretly not knowing to others my purpose".

"Ok … as you wish", the chief left the place. Roberts lit a cigar and watched Mathews was coming nearby.

"So Mr. Roberts, is there any clue about the killer?"

"No officer, you are the incharge of the case … You should know more information than me".

"Roberts … you are a clever man. I know the chief assigned the project to you … Don't bluff me".

Roberts smiled, but he didn't give any reply to Mathews.

CHAPTER III

THE ADVENTUROUS JOURNEY

Manchester Piccadilly Train Station. Evening 6 P.M.

Passengers were moving busily one platform to another platform. It is the principal railway station in Manchester. It has 14 platforms. The retail shops in the station filled with the crowds. Kevin stood nearby a book shop with his luggage. He is waiting for some one.

"Kevin…", a lady addressed him. He raised his head and his lips opened with surprise "Wow! What a surprise.",

"I can't believe it." The lady exclaimed.

"Is it true? Elisa… unbelievable".

"Ya…", Elisa agreed. "It is true".

Kevin was handsome from the depth of his eyes to the gentle expressions of his voice. He had tousled dark brown hair, which was thick and lustrous. His mesmerizing deep ocean blue eyes talks so much. His perfect lips ripe for the kissing. His strong muscled hands attract girls. He is a man of any girl's dream.

"There is no change in you", Elisa admired him. Kevin smiled and took her hand.

"I missed your great friendship these days." He said.Elisa was silent. She remembered her college days. The two were the students of 'London school of Economics'.

"Where are you now?" she asked him.

"I stay in London and work for 'Venture Economics', one of the leading Economics consultancies".

"Wow! That is great", Elisa watched him adminingly, "Are you waiting for someone?".

"Ya… My fiancy … Isabella".

"Kevin… Are you engaged?", she questioned.

"Yes… I am engaged with my subordinate, Isabella. She also works for the same company. Next month I am going to marry her."

"Hi Kevin,"A beautiful lady voice greeted him.

"Hi Isabella," Kevin eyes sparkled watching her.

Elisa stunned watching her beauty. Her tall frame and slender body were like a model. Her blue eyes, like the sea, were calm and emotionless. Long, wavy blonde hair, so smooth and silky, almost as if it was tailored from gold fabric. Her pastel white skin which made her beautiful pink lips stand out. Her cheeks were rouged and she was dressed in a pair of blue skinny jeans and a white band shirt.

Elisa hid her feelings of jealous.

"Gorgeous you are", Kevin admired her.

"By the way… She is Elisa, my college mate." Kevin introduced Elisa to Isabella.

"Elisa… Elisa Peter", she offered her hand.

"Isabella… Isabella Jones".

"Elisa… where are you going on now?"

"I have a trip to coverly hills".

"Oh! Great… we are also coming", Kevin exclaimed.

Suddenly, there is an announcement. "All the passengers of 'Coverly hills expedition' are requested to reach platform no.2. Thank you".

"Let us move to platform No.2", Kevin said.

"It is a thrilling and adventurous journey… throughout the world, people who like adventures want to explore Coverly hills… Do you know, once in 5 years 'Manchester Club' organizes the Expedition. My friends told me that it would be a dangerous to travel Coverly hills. But, you know, I love adventures", Isabella was explaining. Elisa with a smile was listening to what she is explaining.

"Hey Kevin…", loud shout of a man echoed the station.

"Jack...Ha...Ha...again man after so many years". Kevin exclaimed happily.

A twenty eight years old guy with great muscles wearing black shorts with a brown shirt ran to Kevin and hugged him. Kevin introduced girls.

"Jack... This is Isabella, my fiancy and that is Elisa, my college mate".

"Hi girls", Jack greeted them, "Isabella... you look awesome".

Elisa eyes jealously watched Isabella. She watched time. It is 6.50 PM. Most of the passengers of Expedition are arriving and waiting for the train. Most of the travellers are from different countries. The platform No.2 is very colourful with colourfully dressed people representing their tradition and culture.

Time 7 PM...

passengers are eagerly waiting for the train. Finally the train arrived. 'The train of Coverly hills expedition' looks like a wonder to all the passengers.

It is a luxurious train, completely with huge glass windows, 5 star meals, decked bars and more. It is a delight in its own right, the joy of watching hills, meadows, castles, water falls roll by while travelling through coverly hills, as you sit tucked in delightly comfortable cabin is the experience of life time. There is a blend of comfort, luxury with adventurous journey. The train travels through scenic landscape through coverly hills explores natural wonders. This train journey is the perfect dream of everyone who love nature and adventures.

There is an announcement.

"All the passengers who are travelling 'Coverly hills expedition' are welcomed by Manchester Club Organisation. It is a great journey of life time. Every two members have been given a cabin to enjoy with all the facilities… every compartment has 6 cabins… you will be provided with a dining room. Doctors are available for Medical emergency… The train is covered with tight security and we hope you enjoy the trip much. Thank you".

"Hey… we all are allotted to compartment No.2".

"All… It is unbelievable", Isabella said.

"Yes… we can enjoy the trip…come on…let us get in", saying that Kevin lead the group to compartment.

The compartment is very spacious at 240 sq.ft. with glass windows. There are 6 separate cabins with sleeping space, a dedicated sitting area with dressing tables. The travelers can go to dining car for food (or) order it to the compartment. They will enjoy snappy service, excellent food and beverage service throughout the train. Fresh ingredients and fine wine enhance the dining experience. All guests receive complimentary use of bath robes, towels, slippers and luxury toiletries. There is a facility of a shower bath. The deluxe facilities of the compartment mesmorized everyone.

The group reached compartment No.2. on notice board, there are twelve names. Kevin read them loudly.

"Jack Dorson, Roberts, Isabella, Briganzo, Rachel, Kevin, Raman, Madhavi, Elisa, Antonio, Caremon, Sherlocks".

"O.K… Come on man… Let us go", Jack advised Kevin.

They entered the compartment with their luggage.

"Wow, it is beautiful", entering the compartment Isabella exclaimed.

The lavished perfume gave pleasure to them. They settled in their allotted cabins.

The remaining passengers came one by one with their luggages. Roberts is one among them in the compartment No.2. There was an attendant to the compartment. Suddenly there was an announcement.

"Ladies and Gentlemen… Welcome to the adventurous journey of Coverly hills… the trip gives you not only thrilling experiences but also feast to eyes with naturstic scenic beauty… the train is going to start at 8 PM. Thank you".

Elisa has shared her cabin with Sherlocks.

"Is it convenient for you", Sherlocks asked her.

"Ya… It's ok", she said.

"By the way I am Sherlocks, from Germany".

"Hi Sherlocks… This is Elisa from London".

The train started slowly... It is picking up speed... everyone was busy adjusting their luggage... Elisa kept her luggage under her sleeping bed... very spacious cabin it is... she has less luggage, barely a bag.

Sherlocks has a lot of list with him and he was very busy counting them. Elisa took a book from her bag and sat by the window side. The train gathered speed. Suddenly there was a knock on the door.

"Yes, come on", Sherlocks permitted. Kevin entered, "After 10 minutes, we have a gathering in my cabin for all our compartmental mates".

"Ya, surely I will come", Elisa replied. Sherlocks also agreed to it. He was very busy adjusting his luggage.

"You brought heavy luggage", Elisa asked him.

"Ya...you know I don't want to take any risk. We are going to deep forest. We are in need of all the tools and accessories...torch light... heavy long boots... gloves, caps, masks, ...",

Elisa was listening to his words interestingly... He was a tall, lean man with different English accent. He wore a short and yellow tea-shirt.

        "Welcome to my cabin everyone", Kevin started his speech. All the passengers of the compartment came Kevin cabin. Everyone was enthusiastic. "Firstly I would like to ask to introduce himself the older one in our compartment, Roberts". All clapped.

Roberts stood there and watched the young adults in the cabin. "Hi everyone, this is Roberts, GHOST HUNTER". Everyone shocked and watched him with interest.

"Yes, what you have heard about me is right. I am doing research on ghosts".

"Very interesting", Briganzo said.

"Strange", Jack sasid.

"You know, There are ghosts in the train", Roberts slowly proclaimed.

"Are you joking old man?," Briganzo asked him.

"No, I am telling you the truth, Every five years once, Manchester Club organizes the trip. You know, every time at least 4 members suspiciously killed on the trip. These are the paper cuttings. No one knows who have killed them. They have been killed mysteriously". All took paper cuttings of old news papers and were reading them. Elisa took a paper interestingly and read it.

"You know... mostly women have been killed", Roberts proclaimed with authenticative voice.

Caremon took the hand of Antonio, her boy friend. They both were from Switzerland. Antonio kept his hand around her and said, "No problem... I am with you".

"It is the work of ghosts... surely I will catch them in my camera this year".

A camera was hanging around his neck. He wore shorts

and dark blue T-shirt.

Then Briganzo said, "Hi, This is Briganzo from Africa. She is my wife Rachel from Australia. We are recently married couple, when I was in Australia, we were class-mates. After that, we became good friends. we were in Relationship nearly 3 years then we understood each other and got married.I only suggested her this adven-turous trip. And it is our first outing, just like this is our honey moon". Every one clapped and congratulated them.

"By completion of the trip, you should have a baby". Jack dorson commented. All laughed and Rachel's face blushed in red colour with shy.

"Hey, you couple look like from India, Am I right?", Kevin asked Raman.

"Ya, my dear friends… we are couple from India… my-self is Raman and she is Madhavi, my wife. We got mar-ried two years back. I love adventurous journeys, So, we are here to travel with you".

All introduced themselves and Kerin finally brought out a champagne bottle to celebrate the party. Isabella served all.

"Cheers!", saying that. All sipped the drink of cham-pagne. Kevin opened his music studio. The big sound of old beatles changed the environment.

"Great music to listen", Madhavi said all were dancing and enjoying. The train was moving with its great speed. All were enjoying, but they don't know what they are going to face...

CHAPTER IV

THE DEATH FOREST

Noris check point,
Morning 6 A.M.

The train stopped to get clearance... The beautiful early sun rays touched every compartment... The wind blowing from the hills give immense pleasure who gotdown the train. The hills before their very eyes stood like the unconquered king sat on a thrown to rule. It is the starting point of the hills. There onwards, the journey is through meadows, waterfalls and thickly densed forest.

"All the passengers are requested to get in the train to continue their beautiful journey... Thank you". Listening to the announcement Isabella woke up.

"Hi, good morning", Kevin greeted her.

"Good morning, where are we now?", she asked him.

"Noris check point, here onwards Coverly hills start",

he replied.

She watched the beautiful scenery through the glass window. The flowers of different varieties with early beautiful snow drops greeted her. She opened the glass window, the chilly wind touched her face gently.

"Wow!", she admired the early morning nature. The train resumed its journey. There was a knock on the door. "Come in!" Kevin replied. The attendant entered with two cups of auromatic hot coffee.

"Keep them on the table", Kevin said.

The attendant kept the cups on the table and left.

"Have it!" Kevin gave a cup to her. She took the cup and enjoyed the beautiful smell of coffee.

"May I come in!" Elisa entered without their reply. She was ready!

"Hi Elisa, got ready early in the morning. Where do you want to go!"

"Just making a round in the train. Going to dining car, having breakfast and meeting new friends".

"Great!", Kevin exclaimed.

"Ok. Bye", saying that she left the cabin.

The train was moving on and it affords the panoramic views of pine forests, valleys. "The greatest journey I ever had", Kevin said.

"Ya... It's amazing", sitting near by window. Isabella said.

Finally, the train reached its first camp. There is an announcement.

"Good morning everyone… All the passengers are requested to get off the train with their luggage… Thank you".

Passengers one by one got off the train… Roberts watched the time. It was 8 o' clock. He watched the place curiously.

It was a beautiful place with thick pine trees which are very high. It was drizzing. There is no station, just there is a point. It was a thickly dense forest area.

Vehicles are waiting for passengers to take them into the deep forest.

"Come on Roberts… move", said Kevin.

"Ya…", saying that, he moved to a vehicle. Suddenly he felt discomfort. Someone was observing him secretly. He got into a van and sat by a window seat. All his compartment mates got into the same van. All were very busy chit-chatting among themselves. Raman sat by him and placed his hands around his neck and said", come on… old man… let us have great experience".

Roberts smiled, "Thank you young man," There is a chill in the wind. The van started.

The van was moving on a narrow path… Nearly six vans followed it. It was a beautiful place. With a small dirty road. All the vans are moving through the thickest forest. There is a little fog with darkness. The van drivers switched on lights.

"Wow!", says Rachel. "It's thrilling".

"Ya", said Briganzo. The touching of Rachel made him romantic. He took her face in his hands and kissed her. Suddenly Rachel felt uneasy. She felt that some one was observing her. She turned her head and watched Jack. He was eating 'A Dark Chocolate' and watching the pair interestingly. When he saw that she was observing him, he turned his head otherside.

"Come on Elisa," Kevin invited. Elisa who sat in the back seat, came front by Kevin.

"So… what did you do after leaving the college?"

Elisa replied, "Nothing … I did travelling to explore new world".

"Sounds interesting", he said.

Isabella was watching them. May be she hasn't liked the way Kevin behaves with Elisa.

Suddenly there was a small drizzling. The smell of different varieties of flowers give a pleasant experience to everyone. Finally, the vans reached the place where the passengers stay.

There are tree houses on the branches of matured trees… excellently architected with good space.

"Here is your hut sir..", attendant showed Kevin and Isabella the way. For every two members they have allotted a hut.

"Not bad…", Kevin said after entering the hut. There is a place to take bath also.

"Hmm", exclaimed Isabella.

There is a knock on the door. Kevin opened the door. It was attendant!

"Sir, you should get ready in an hour! We should go for sight seeing!"

"I have to bath first", Isabella said bending her body to Kevin. The Fragrance of Jasmin from her body tempted him.

'Let us have shower together", Kevin asked her with husky voice.

"Hmm… naughty", Isabella moaned. He closed the door and took her into his hands… His muscles pressed her body to him.

All are ready to explore the place… The hills are steep… The forest is thick… Really it is an adventurous trip. Everyone was enthusiastically waiting outside.

"Good morning ladies and gentlemen… I hope you are enjoying the trip… I am Austin, the chief of the tour. The adventurous journey of coverly hills has been started in 1895 by my great grandfather 'Sr. Austin'. He was a great explorer of naturalistic world.

We established a club named 'Manchester Club', the prestigious club in London. Every five years we conduct a tour to the people who are passionate to face adventures. Though the tour is risky, with the great support of adventures people we have been running the tour nearly for 125 years.

Austin stopped and watched the gathering. "Today on this auspicious occasion, we are going to conduct 'a challenge' here. Are you ready?" he sounded enthusiastically.

"Ya...", All shouted.

"O.K... We have hid a 'painting of coverly hills' nearby surroundings. If you find it... You will get 10,000/- dollars.

"Wow... that is great", Madhavi said.

"Now the time is 9 A.M... You have been given 2 hours time to find it. The time starts now", he said.

"But, I am giving you a serious warning. Some travellers died previously while exploring the forest here... It is a dangerous place... Don't go deep... If anyone is not interested... They can go for sightseeing with the protection of our guards".

20 members named for competition. Most of the travelers wanted to be safe. They want to reach home safely.

Kevin, Isabella, Roberts, Jack, Elisa, Antonio, Briganzo, Rachel are participating in the game.

"Wow... This is amazing", Rachel said.

"I want to be adventurous", Isabella admiringly said.

Jack said, "Yes, I also want to be adventurous".

The game started. They have been given clues to find

the spot.

All are going on in a different way taking clues…

It is densly vegetated area… trees are very high covering that they haven't allowed the sun to fall its rays .Going through the forest is not an easy… birds are making vivid sounds… The foot steps of travellers distracted them…

"This way", Elisa guided them. Watching the first clue.

"No… This way", Isabella replied. Kevin got confused and examined the clue. "Elisa may be right… That's way".

"But… all are going this way", Isabella cried impatiently. She hasn't liked the way Elisa behaves.

"No… Elisa is very clever… believe her." The words made Isabella jealous of Elisa. "If I get chance… I will leave you in the forest" she murmured. Kevin observed her feelings and smiled. 'No woman likes her fiancy praises the other girl". Roberts was silently followed them.

The four were moving in different direction.

The long pine trees obstructed the sun rays to fall… There is darkness there… The thick vegetation of the forest obstructed them moving fast. They are trying to walk watching the clue map. They can here the sound of the footsteps on the dry leaves. Kevin in one hand took a torch and wore a bag on his back. They can hear the sound of water falling faintly… Suddenly there was silence… There is no sound of birds.

"Hush!", Kevin stopped all. "Do you know... last time my friend came here... He saw a ghost moving". Isabella frightened hearing the words of Roberts. She went near by Kevin taking his hand in her hands.

To remember the way they came, Kevin was dropping some coloured stones on the way. There was a strange sound from near by bushes. Suddenly a wolf came on their way... The ferocious wolf showed its jaws and ready to attack.

"Hush! Be silent", whispered Kevin.

All stood silently.

"Do you have a lighter?", Kevin asked Roberts.

"Here it is!", he has given it to him.

He lit the lighter and showing it to the wolf, he made a loud cry. Wolf turned back and disappeared in the bushes.

Clouds covered the sky... They have torches in their hands... Isabella lighted her torch.

"It is strange that there is no noise here... generally we can here the sounds of birds and animals.

"Because of ghosts", Roberts said.

Suddenly there is a sudden sound of someone running near by.

"Hush... Someone is there", said Roberts.

Kevin torched there. There is a thick bush. They waited a minute. No sound.

"Don't be fearful Roberts… It is a safe jone", Kevin said.

All are ready to move, but they heard clearly someone moving… The sound of heavy steps on dry leaves. Elisa shivered, "Who is there?", her voice is trembling. The sound stopped. Suddenly the rain started heavily. They wore rain coats hurriedly.

"Let us move… May be an animal", Isabella cooled all with her words. The rain was pouring. Full darkness covered the area. All lit torches. Kevin is leaving all. All are moving hand in hand.

"It is impossible to complete the task in this weather… Let us move to our camp back". Isabella cried loudly, the ravishing wind is throwing them aside.

It is very difficult to return. They were moving together.

"My friend told me there were ghosts here. They had seen them… I want to stay here now", Roberts words made Kevin astonished.

"What old man… Do you want to die here". The rain is pouring like that they can't see one another. They were moving slowly.

Suddenly a white shadow appears at the far end… They can clearly see in the darkness. They stopped with fear. The blowing sound of the wind through trees, the darkness of the forest, the fearful shadow made Elisa tremble and took the hand of Kevin in her hand.

"No need to fear… It is an illusion", but no one believed his words. Even he also didn't believe that it was an illusion.

Roberts feels like it is a dream.Instead of fearing, he said, "My dream has come true". The white shadow is moving slowly towards the north and disappeared.

Kevin sighed and relieved. 'O.K. let us move", hurriedly he was leading them. The rain is pouring steadily. They were in a hurry-suddenly a scream of a woman shocked everyone. "Oh! My god," Isabella frightened and tears were rolling from her eyes... she cried.

"Where is Elisa?" Roberts shocked.

"Help me Kevin... Isabella. Help me", the loud cries of a woman alerted them.

"That is Elisa", Roberts moved hurriedly to the sound side. They can't see what is there before because of thick, high bushes. There is a long grass covered everywhere. The rain, the darkness was obstructing them to move fast... Torch lights lighting is unable to pierce the darkness.

Isabella's face became pale with fear, her body is trembling.

"No... Don't kill me... please... leave me", the words of Elisa shocked everyone.

Kevin cried, "Elisa... Where are you?". "Are you O.K.?"

"Oh my God!", Isabella was trembling.

"Elisa...", Kevin cried. But there is no reply. The rain subsided.

"That way", Roberts lead everyone on the way of sound.

"Kevin... come here", Isabella cried. There were blood stains. Isabella cried watching the blood. "No...", It made her fully frighten.

Kevin took the hand of Isabella in his hand taking her nearer.

In the torch light lighting, they moved forward. Roberts focused torch light lighting on the blood stains and walking slowly...

Suddenly there is a big tree appeared before his eyes... It has big roots. At the root of the tree, Watching the scene, Isabella started making loud screams.

It was horrible... Elisa throat was cut... blood was coming out... her legs and hands were tied... eyes were wide open with fear. There was blood shed... on her forehead, it was written with a knife.

"I AM YOUR KILLER".

Isabella was unstoppably screaming. Those screams made the forest resounded. Kevin tried to comfort her. Roberts unmoved.

Suddenly they heard a sound of someone coming. The guards covered the place.

"Sir! I am Sam, chief security officer. You can go now, we will take care of it".

Kevin is unwilling to leave the place. But with heavy heart, he left the place with Isabella. Roberts followed them.

CHAPTER V

VINTAGE CAVES

Isabella... Open your eyes".
Isabella tried to open her eyes... that's Kevin's voice.

"Where are we?"

"In the hut... we are safe... on the way of return, you fainted".

Tears were rolling on her cheeks... she didn't believe what she saw... The dead body of Elisa frightened her... She was in utter disappointment and distress.

"I want to quit the tour", Isabella.

Kevin was silent. Roberts entered the cabin. "Is it possible to quit the tour now?, It's impossible". He said quietly.

"Isabella... O.K. we have come here to do adventurous journey... but you know... It is unfortunate incident happened".

"But… who kills like that".

"A psycho killer…",

"How can you say?"

"A psycho killer only can kill like that".

"How can he come here… It is the deepest forest".

"May be, someone in the passengers is psycho-killer".

"Excuse me", a voice from outside.

"Sorry to disturb you… This is 'Sam', security officer. He was in a black long coat wearing round hat on his head.

"Nice to meet you officer", Kevin remarked. Sam smiled and asked, "Can you explain what happened when you went to the forest". Kevin explained everything. Roberts was silent. Sam turned to Roberts and asked him.

"Sir, I have seen you somewhere".

Roberts was silent. He didn't give any reply.

"What was the white shadow?", Sam asked.

"May be a traveler was going on his way with lighting", Kevin replied.

"No… that is not the satisfactory answer… Something fishy in it".

The attendant came there, "Sir, time to leave the place". "Ya… OK", Kevin replied.

◆ ◆ ◆

Second destination,

'Vintage caves'

The train was moving on... everyone in the train was not in mood... They got fear of 'The psycho-killer'.

Jack, Sherlocks, Briganzo, Rachel, Raman and Madhavi gathered at a table in the dining car. They were silent. Sherlocks remembered Elisa...

"How sweet she was", He sighed. Jack patted his back. 'How cruelly she was killed', Rachel commented.

"Hi!", Roberts joined the party. "We have come here to enjoy... not to sit sad," he advised them.

"To come out of the mood, we have to order for drinks". The dining car was very busy with passengers. It was the spacious one. The waiters were very busy with taking orders. The melodious music of piano suits the environment.

Roberts observed the crowd. No one looked suspicious. All are behaving naturally. 'Sir... your coffee", waiter brought it.

"Thank you", saying that he sipped it. The taste of it vibrated his body. 'I like it', saying this, he took out a cigar.

"Excuse me", saying that, he tried to go to smoking

zone. Suddenly he found to a lace of the boot loosened. He bent to tie. He heard a noise of releasing a weapon to attack. Without raising his head, he looked at. Everything was normal. He tied his lace and slowly straightened. He found a sharp steel made weapon with sharp edge on the wooden cover. He took out his gloves from his pocket and wore them. He took out the weapon carefully and kept it in a plastic bottle. No one observed it, except Madhavi.

"Uncle, what happened", she asked him. "Nothing my child", he replied with a smile and examined the dining car. Everything was calm and there was nothing suspicious.

"Clever man he is!", Roberts murmurbed. He knew that the killer had recognized him. He was trying to kill him also.

Madhavi was such a woman who was very fearful and anxious. After the incident of Elisa, she pressured Raman to quit the trip... But Raman convinced her that it would be the personal affair of Elisa lead to tragic end of her life.

"Uncle... tell me... what happened", Madhavi pressured him. Everyone was silent and asked her what happened.

"Ladies and Gentlemen... you know. I am a ghost hunter... but you should believe my words".

"Surely uncle... tell me", Briganzo forwarded with interest.

"No... you shouldn't believe my words after hearing my words".

"No... we surely believe", Raman said.

"Then listen to me carefully... Last night when I was with the group of Kevin, I saw a white shadow moving there".

"I heard the same from Kevin", Jack supported him. Madhavi eyes became wide open with fear.

Roberts continued, "My friend also saw the same ghost five years back in the same trip. He told me that, when he saw the ghost, that day also a woman was killed brutally". All were listening to it interestingly. Rachel took the hand of Briganzo in her hand with fear.

"The same ghost today now in this dining car 5 minutes back attacked me to kill", he told them slowly.

Madhavi was trembling... She was in traditional dress of India i.e., saree.

"Yes, it attacked me and this is the evidence", he showed the plastic bottle.

The small weapon in the plastic bottle increased their curiosity.

"I don't believe ghosts", Jack said.

"But I believe!," Madhavi replied. Raman didn't speak anything.

"Gentleman, it is not the matter to play jokes. I think we are in danger zone. The killer is with us in the train,

No doubt about it", Sherlocks expressed his opinion.

"O.K. I have to leave now, Good day all of you", saying that Roberts left.

"Vintage Caves'

'Vintage Caves', one of the longest caves in the world. The cave formation began when Acid rain is absorbed by the ground. Acid rain consists of rainwater mixed with carbon dioxide. As this acid rain travels through the ground. It comes in contact with solid rocks. If this rock is made of limestone (or) dolomite, the water will react chemically until it slowly dissolves the rock and hollow space is formed. As the space becomes bigger, water begins to flow through it, eventually creating a stream (or) under ground river. At this point, erosion and weathering begin and further cave formation. After a thousand years, the hollow space is already big enough for a human to enter. After a million years, chambers and columns form due to erosion and we can see spectacular caves.

All were enthusiastic to visit caves. But the death of Elisa made them back. Raman is very much interested, but Madhavi not. She has the fear of the killer… May be he would arrive. Raman didn't care for it. He felt that she had been killed on her personal reasons.

Madhavi has the view of the killer, but Raman rejected it saying that it is the trick of the authorities to make the journey adventurous. Madhavi didn't believe his words. Raman dragged her nearer, "Oh... come on Madhavi... There is no problem... I am here with you", saying that he took her at the entrance of the cave. Antonio, Caremon, Kevin, Isabella have also showed interest to watch the caves. Jack hasn't shown interest, but Roberts convinced him to go on to the caves.

After entering in it, Robert felt chilled... The fearful environment in the caves make fearful any courageous man. It has so many ways to go... There are so many chambers... Raman ran in a way... Madhavi followed him.

"Sir, you should be careful in the caves. It has taken so many people lives". The words are repeating in her mind frequently.

Madhavi tightened her hand around him and he watched into her eyes. The touch of her body in the cold weather made him romantic. Without caring his feelings, she is coming with him.

It is the cave of ancient sculptures, sunlight is entering through the holes of top of the cave.

"Come this way", Raman showed her a way.

"Most of the people are going that way", Madhavi pointed.

"But we go this way", Raman thought was different.

Old ancient walls of the cave are very artistic... They have torches with them... The chambers are little dark... Suddenly Raman stopped "Hey... look at..."

There is a small narrow way "We go through this way…" Raman remarked.

"No… it is dangerous", Madhavi refused.

"No problem… I am here", dragging her near to him, he started moving on the way.

"Raman!" she denied.

But he took her to a place which is spacious! There is an ancient sculpture which is romantic!

Madhavi stared at it opening her mouth.

"Beautiful…", Raman whispered in her ears. She suddenly tried to run back, but Raman opposed it taking her waist into his both hands.

"No…", Madhavi moaned with sweet pain.

Without asking her permission, he touched her back with his hands. Madhavi turned round and closed her eyes. Raman kissed her with ecstacy.

"Raman… you naughty", Madhavi whispered in his ears. Her saree dropped. Like snakes, their bodies are moving to… His lips are touching somewhere of her body. Suddenly a small sound of stones falling…

Madhavi alerted, "Someone is coming…". But Raman was unable to hear. He was very busy with her body and his lips were touching the deep of her body.

"Wow!", A rough voice of someone made them conscious. Raman left Madhavi and asked her "Have you heard a noise?", Madhavi didn't get a word. Just then…

'BANG', Raman doesn't know what happened.

There was a pain in the head... Blood was running on the neck... he can listen to the cries of Madhavi.

"No...", Raman tried to open his eyes. He didn't get the chance. 'I wanna kill you... I wanna kill you'. There was the humming sound with a different voice. He can't open his eyes.

"Hush...Lady...my darling. If you make a noise... then", the words made her silent.

"Sat there", he ordered.

She sat silently. Raman was in blood shed. Her mental condition is different. She was staring at the killer... wearing a mask... in a black long coat...

The killer went near to Raman. Taking a knife, "What to do...?" He whispered in the ears of Raman. Raman was unable to move... blood was running from his head.

"What to do Madam... with him", the words of killer made her tremble.

"Please... leave us".

"Hmm... Do one thing... You kill him and I will leave you...".

"No... I won't", Madhavi screamed.

"BANG...", the hammer touched her head also.

"I don't like your reply", saying that again the killer threw the hammer on... It missed her.

"Oh... escaped... OK", he was ready to go near to her. He

heard the sounds of foot steps far away.

"O.K, bye," saying that he took his knife out.

The screams of Raman and Madhavi resounded the cave.

Sam reached the spot hurriedly after hearing the news.

"Sir…", the guards at the spot saluted him. He watched the scene of offence. It was horrible… They were beaten with hammer, stabbed with a knife… There was blood shed. Madhavi fore head was engraved with

"I AM YOUR KILLER".

Austin's chamber in the train

The train was going on its way… "May I come in sir", "Yes", Austin replied. Sam got into the room. Austin silently watched him.

"Mr. Sam, I have given you the responsibility of security. But, you failed. You should give explanation for it".

"Sir… I have taken so many precautions not to happen unwanted incidents. But, there is no cooperation of the travellers. They didn't follow my instructions. I have asked them to be in a group. If they go individually means what should I do?"

"Mr. Sam, I don't consider your words of consolation. You are a responsible person, you should come with a plan of action. It shouldn't be repeated in future. You can go now".

"O.K. Sir", saying that he saluted Austin and left the place.

All the travellers were in utter confusion... they were in horror... some asked the officials to go back.

"We request all the passengers to go back to their seats... We are going to take all the precautionary measures for the safety of the passengers.

In compartment No. 2, all sat together... They were silent.

Briganzo exclaimed with a sigh "How horrible!"

"Ya... we lost three members in the same compartment...", Jack sadly exclaimed.

"In the same compartment...", Kevin said.

"Something is fishy!" he said.

"Why three members died from the same compartment?," Isabella questioned herself.

"How brutally they have been killed!", exclaimed Caramen.

"Ghost!! It is the work of the ghost only... No newsperson can enter this place...".

"Ghost!" Caremon horrified.

She has belief in ghosts... "Have you seen it?"

Robert enthusiastically forwarded "Ya! A ghost... I had

seen it before Elisa's horrible murder… It wore a white dress and was wandering in the forest area. The same ghost killed Raman and Madhavi." It is leaving its Mark 'I AM YOUR KILLER'.

Caremon opened her mouth wide open with fear. Antonio took her nearer to him.

"Are you a kid?… How can you believe ghosts?"

"Gentleman… It is true… ghosts can't hide any where… They are with us".

"I can't understand", Antonio replied. "You can understand my words in future", saying that, he left the place. All watched him silently.

CHAPTER VI

THE DEVIL'S SPOT

Kevin opened his eyes. Isabella said, "Get up Kevin... We should be ready...".
"Reached our destination?...", Kevin asked.

"Ya... This is the third camp... We should walk atleast 3 kms from here to reach our camp. 'The devil's spot'.

"Hmm...", said Kevin.

"Hurry up...", she said, "We shouldn't be late. We should go in a group so that we could...", she stopped.

"We could...", asked Kevin.

"We could escape from the killer... You know",

Kevin got up from bed and went to the mirror. He saw his face in the mirror.

"Something strange is happening to my body...", He exclaimed.

Isabella saw him strangely, "I found some strange things with you".

"What…", Kevin said.

"See… this dress… the black coat," He saw it. "No… It is not mine". "I found a dark chocolate in it". She stressed. Kevin became silent and went nearer to her".

"Do you believe that I am the killer", Kevin asked her.

"I don't mean…", Isabella said. Suddenly there was a knock on the door.

"Sir… Time to leave", attendant reminded them. Kevin took her nearer to him and said "My dear queen… I amn't the killer, but you are the killer". She was silent and suddenly said, "O.K… get ready".

"I don't want to go… I want to stay here", Caremon said.

"Why…", Antonio said, "We should go in a group… then there is no fear of killer…" said Antonio, "If we stay here… may be he attacks us. Let us go".

Roberts who is watching the scene is silent. He is behavving like that he knows everything.

"I guess… in our compartment only the killer is". Roberts murmured in the ears of Briganzo.

Briganzo said slowly "May be you are the killer". Roberts laughed loudly… "Ya… you are right man… I am also…", his brown eyes sparkled. Isabella was listening to their words silently. Finally all got down from compartment No. 2.

◆ ◆ ◆

It is a beautiful spot… There are so many water-falls around them. So many tree species within a small area… The thickness of vegetation gave a feast to the people… Early morning fog chilled their body.

"Beautiful…", murmurbed Isabella, "I have never seen such a beautiful place".

The sounds of different bird species gives immense pleasure to everyone.

"Beautiful", Jack said.

'Ya!', exclaimed Sherlocks.

"Let us move…", Kevin said.

All are moving to… Guards are observing all giving instructions to them.

"Hi!", caremon greeted Isabella.

"Hi! Let us move as a group".

"Sure!", the travelers of compartment No. 2 are moving in a group side by side.

Caremon is moving with Antonio hand in hand forgetting their fear.

"How romantic the place is!" she said. "Ya! Untouched by civilized people".

The long high different varieties of tree species are observing the rays of the sun to fall.

"Be careful...", warned Mathews watching the thick vegetation on the way... people are moving in groups.

Suddenly a loud cry of a woman stopped the heart beat of all...

"Oh my God!...", Isabella frightened.

Tears were rolling in the eyes of Rachel. She was murmuring 'It is a mistake... It is a mistake' Briganzo is unmoved.

"Help me...No...Help me," the cries of a woman are very loud.

"I go and watch", Kevin said.

"No... No...", Isabella cried.

"Where are the guards?", asked Caremon.

"They have already gone... ".Austin said.

Roberts suddenly came there... He was back because of walking slowly... He was gasping...", I saw someone there", pointing a way.

"Where are the guards? How can they leave us alone?" Rachel screamed.

"Cool Baby! We are all here". Briganzo consoled her.

"No... It's not right", Rachel said.

"Let us move together", Roberts advised them.

Suddenly Sam with two guards came there. All relieved watching them. "Why are you slow in walking... Why can't you be in the group?"

"Sorry sir for that… we heard screams in the forest".

"Ya… Guards went to find it", Sam replied.

"Come on… Let us move".

They started moving on the way… The guards are protecting them… The way is narrow. "Be careful…", Sam warned the others. Suddenly there was the sound of a tiger roaring… All alerted.

"Stop… don't move". There was utter silence. The thick bushes by the narrow way frighten them… Rachel was in full sweat. There is the sound of foot steps on the leaves.

"Tiger…", one of the guards cried. He tried to fire the gun. "No…", said Sam, but it was too late. The tiger jumped on them roaring. All ran with fear.

"This side…", Kevin told Isabella. Tiger wounded a guard attacking him. Sam hurriedly took his gun and fired pointing on its forehead… The tiger fell moaning on the floor. There is no movement in it, then Guards saw the travelers running.

"Stop…", said Sam "I have killed the tiger… no problem". One by one all came back there.

"Where are Antonio and Caremon?" Roberts asked. There was utter silence.

"Search for them", Sam ordered.guards went on in search for them.

◆ ◆ ◆

"Oh my God...", Caremon exclaimed with fear.

"I can't run", Anotonio stopped.

"How ferocious it is! 9 feet tall. May be the tiger killed all". They reached the place where there was no way... This grass of 6 feet high covered the area... They can't see what is there the other side. 'Let us move', Antonio proposed to her. Suddenly they heard the voice of Sam.

"Hey... no problem... come here", the sound alerted them. Suddenly they heard the sound of water. Caremon asked him to go there. They moved to the side. They reached the place where a brook was flowing. The bluish water flowing like a snake moving fast. Caremon washed her face. The water was chilly and awakened her nerves. Antonio sat on a rock and put his legs into the water. The small fish touched his legs with affection. He felt relieved from his tension.

"Hey... give me the water bottle", Antonio said to Caremon. But Caremon was unmoved. Her eyes become wide open.

"Antonio...", she warned him, but it was too late. There was a blow on the head of Antonio.

"BANG" Antonio's eyes blushed. There was blood covering his eyes... He fell down. Caremon was ready to move.

"No...", said the killer, "If you move... I will kill Antonio". He was with the hammer in his hand.

"No…", Caremon was pleading,

"Don't kill him. Leave us…" requested voice of her unmoved the killer. He took a knife out. Caremon eyes were wide open watching the scene. "No… leave him!", she cried. But it was too late. The brutal using of knife made there blood shed.

"Help… Help", screaming like a mad girl, she started running.

But she slipped and fainted.

she opened her eyes. she didn't know where she was. It was one of the most magnificent caves. She wants to move… but she was unable to move… Her hands and legs were tied… Her mouth was taped… She heard the foot steps of some one…

"Waiting for this time", killer came near to her silently… "You are…", Caremon doubtedly questioned the killer. He was in blue coat eating a dark chocolate.

"Ya… you recognized me Caremon", said the killer calmly.

"No… It is impossible… How close you are to me… No one believes that you are the killer". Tears were rolling from her eyes.

"I don't like sentiments caremon… I hate people" Caremon was trying to escape. The killer took out his knife and cut the rope of her legs. She stood and tried to ran.

"Ha...Ha...Ha..., come on... come on my baby... Where are you going?." The killer followed her. She ran through the trees, but she found the dead end... There is a deep valley before her.

"Oh my dear... You can't escape from here...".

"Leave me please", she pleaded.

"Shh... The typical sound of the killer frightened her... He took her hand in his hand... The screams of her resounded the forest.

Sam and guards ran to the way of the sound. They found the dead body of Antonio by brook side.

Hurriedly they reached the top of the hill. They found the dead body of Caremon... Her hands were tied... There were several wounds on her body... Her eyes were wide open with horror... One of the guards vomited watching the blood shed. Again there was a writing on the forehead

"I AM YOUR KILLER".

CHAPTER VII

HILL TOP WATER FALLS

Austin's Chamber
10 P.M.

Austin was impatient... The brutal killings of travelers made him restless... This is the first time there are serial killings. Previously, there were accidental deaths. Sam was called on.

Sam entered silently. There was silence between them.

"So...", Austin finally broke the silence.

"I am taking responsible for my failure sir... I am resigning to my post".

Austin was silent... He offered a cigar to Sam. Sam didn't believe it... Generally Austin is reserved. Today his behavior is totally different.

"Sam... can I ask you a question?", Austin suddenly asked him.

"Sure sir", he said.

"All the people believe that you are helping the killer". Austin slowly blew the bomb. But Sam didn't react. He laughed and said, "Sir, this is not the mistake of passengers. This is the mistake of mine. My question here is 'Do you believe that sir?" Austin didn't reply.

"Sam... You can go now", Austin said "What about my resignation sir", he asked. "I don't accept it, when the time comes, I will tell you. At least, from now onwards we shouldn take care of our passengers. Our journey shouldn't be a mess".

"O.K. Sir, I will do it", he left Austin's cabin hurriedly. The security guard outside of Austin's cabin saluted him.

"Why killer targeted compartment No. 2", Isabella questioned. All the members in compartment 2 gathered in Kevin's cabin. There was no reply.

Emila, Raman, Madhavi, Antonio, Caremon... all are from this compartment.

"Because I guess the killer is one among us", Briganzo replied.

"Then why... why should he kill one by one", Isabella asked.

Kevin silently gave the answer, "For the sake of pleasure and fame."

"Pleasure and fame!", Rachel wondered.

"Ya... psycho killers don't have any base for killing... They try to kill the people for their pleasure and they expect the others have to discuss about them.

"Guys... whatever it may be... we should be careful ourselves... No one protects us except ourselves. If you believe someone comes and protects, It is our fate", Sherlocks told everyone.

"You are right... so many times we discussed to go as a group... but we sometimes overlooked it..." All were talking except jack.

"I have a doubt on him", Jack murmured with Sherlocks.

"It is impossible in that age to became psycho-killers", Sherlocks replied.

"No man... He said he was a witch craft. May be he was doing his 'pujas' to 'WITCHES'. That's why he was killing all. Recently I visited a 'witch craft'. He told that some would offer their 'sacrifice to WITCHES".

Then Roberts suddenly spoke, "Ladies and Gentleman... In my opinion, the psycho killer is from our compartment only".

"How can you say?", Rachel asked him curiously.

"Because the killer targeted our compartment and he was observing our behavior. He knows how we go, and especially he targeted Mostly couples". Listening to it ,Rachel and Isabella frightened.

"But… I hope I will find him very early", Roberts said.

"How?", Isabella asked him.

"I perform 'puja' today in my cabin. My 'favourite ghost' comes there and tells me the 'psycho killer' name."

"Bullshit man… Don't bluff us… In these days also you believe 'ghosts' means it is rubbish… Don't cheat people playing 'tricks'."

"Young man… in your age, people behave like you only… but sometimes we should believe that 'There is a mystery in the world'."

"O.K. old man… no arguments… guys…bye for now". Everyone left Kevin's cabin. while leaving the cabin, Roberts said, "Kevin, in future I am the only person who will catch the killer". Kevin laughed at him said, "Right sir… Good night".

"Good night", saying this, he left the place.

The train reached the next destination "Hill top water-falls". As per schedule, all the travellers got down the train… The early Sunshine falling on the hills made the area 'Goldy'. The thick vegetation covered the hilly area is giving the pleasurly cool breeze…

"The trip is memorable for me", "In a bad way".Sherlocks said.

Kevin looked at him strangely and turned his head left and said, "Friends… for the safety of ours, we should go together without deviating from any disturbance. All agreed. They started moving with their bags on their back. The greenery of the forest is admirable. Sherlocks remembered how he and his friends in his childhood days were talking about the tales of coverly hills. On the way, the scenic beauty of the silent forest mesmorized all.

"Be careful while going and don't leave the group", warning of the guards made all alert. They came to a place where there was a big waterfall. The thunderous sound of it made everyone forget what happened. The water was falling like a white elephant was jumping from the top of the hill. The rainbow appears like an artist draws a picture on a canvas. Forgetting their position, the passengers are moving to the waterfalls laughing and jumping.

"Wow!", the admiration of the Kevin was unbounded.

All went under the falls and enjoying the touch of water on their head.

"No… I can't come", Rachel said. "I have a fear of water from my child hood days, you go and enjoy. I wait for you here", without second thought Briganzo ran to the waterfalls… he was a god swimmer.

Keeping his bag near by pool, he changed his clothes. The cold chilled water made every nerve of his body active. Rachel stood there and watched the surroundings. Briganzo was enjoying swimming. It makes him lose all his tension of killer.

"Excuse me", it was a familiar voice to Rachel.

"Rachel turned back and wondered "Oh my God! I don't

believe my eyes".

Briganzo watched Rachel was talking with someone. Kevin secretly came his back and tried to push him in water. But Briganzo cleverly escaped and laughed at him and chased him to catch. Kevin tried to escape, but Briganzo caught him. Isabella also joined with them. They were laughing and playing. Suddenly Briganzo looked at the side of Rachel. She was not there! He felt something strange.

He came out of the pool and searched for her. All travelers were in enjoying mood. He couldn't find her there. "Where did she go?". He was in confusion. He found guards there.

"Excuse me... I didn't find my wife Rachel, can you help me in finding her".

The guards told him, "Sure sir, where did you see her last time?"

"When I went to the pool... She was there", showing a place near by waterfalls.

The guards immediately intimated the matter to chief security officer, Sam.

"What!", he exclaimed with disbelief "How it happened?".

"Hurry up guys... Let us move". Hurriedly he went in search for her. Briganzo was in utter confusion, murmuring, "I shouldn't have left her alone."

They were searching for her in the forest... Thick

bushes obstruct their way... Briganzo was a strong man... He was in a hurry... "Hurry up officer...", It was very difficult for them to move forward. The thick bushes are so high that they have to cut the vegetation to move forward. There were five members in the search team. Suddenly there was muddy brown colour water with long trees.

"Where is this water coming from?" Briganzo asked. Sam silently watched the place. It is just like brown blanket covered the area.

"Strange!" Sam murmured himself.

The guards entered the water and walking. Sam and Briganzo followed them. The trees there were silent. Suddenly Briganzo felt something touched his leg. He silently watched it.

"Stop!", Sam asked the others... All stopped there... Briganzo legs were shaking... It is a 'Sucuri', an Olive coloured snake with alternating oval shaped black spots. It is 9 meters long.

"Don't move", Briganzo warned others. It was moving slowly round the Briganzo. He found that it was going to attack him. Sam silently took out his revolver and ready to fix. But Briganzo warned him to be silent. He knows that it has the power of killing all of them in minutes. It slowly rounded its body around Briganzo.

Sam fired it hurriedly. 'No', Briganzo warned him, it was too late. It reacted sharply. It occupied Briganzo in seconds.

"Run up man!", Briganzo advised them. Sam with his guards ran back. Briganzo was helplessly watching the snake. The snake is slowly consuming him. "Bye Rachel", those are the last words of Briganzo.

Sam and guards reached the place where they could find a piece of cloth. There were blood stains to it. There was a sound nearby bush. Suddenly two wolves came out of the bush. The guards fired them without waiting. The cries of wolves resounded the forest.

"Sir, this side", one of the guards shouted. They went there hurriedly. The dead body of Rachel was there in a horrified manner. Her legs were tied. Her body was with small cuts with blood shed... Sam took his revolver out and shot in the air five times. The sound of bullets resounded the forest made everyone frightened. Sam went nearby dead body", 5 minutes back it might happen", saying that he ordered the soldiers to find the killer.

"Boys... let us search for the killer".

The walking sound on dry leaves by guards made monkey watch them curiously. Suddenly they heard the noise of someone running.

All ran towards the sound.

"Sir!", A guard cried hurriedly "There is something back of the tree". They went there. Suddenly a small bear came out and watching them helplessly.

"Oh...come on boys...", Sam exclaimed with anger.

The fearful incidents of the tour worried the authorities. The series of deaths happening there with brutality lacked their hope.

"This is my resignation letter for my failure", Sam handed over the letter to the chairman.

"Sir, I am very unhappy about the incidents happening around me… It is the brutality I have never seen in my life".

The chairman silently accepted the resignation of Sam.

"Gentleman! Now I would like to introduce you the new security officer for our journey! He is coming here now". The chairman said.

"Who is he sir?", Sam asked him.

Then suddenly door bell rang. 'Come in'. Roberts entered the room.

"Meet Mr. Roberts, the chief detective from England".

"Great to see you sir!", Sam greeted him.

"Thank you, Sam", he replied. Last night, your chairman asked my help to catch the killer. I have come here for the same purpose."

"Have you got any clue?"

"Yes, but I have some doubts on it."

"Is he a passenger in the train?"

"I guess the psycho killer is travelling with us. At any time, we catch him with good evidence".

"Sir, I have a doubt. Why the killer targeted compartment No.2".

Roberts laughed and didn't give any clue about it.

"Next stop is the famous 'haunted house'. It is the place where we should be careful about it."

"Sir I guess the killer recognized me and attacked me once when I was in dining room".

"What!" Austin wondered. But you didn't complain about it".

"Sir, may be the killer targeted the couple Kevin and Isabella", Roberts changed the topic.

"Sir, in my opinion the killer should be Kevin. His behavior is strange to me" Sam said.

"No, it is not possible. When Elisa was killed, I was with Kevin." Roberts said. Austin lit his cigar, the clock showed 10 P.M.

"O.K gentlemen, thank you for coming here. Good night".

"Good night sir", saying that Roberts and Sam left the place.

Compartment No.2,

There was utter silence. Sherlocks and Jack were in

total disappointment.

"I guess we are the next target", Isabella said with fear. Kevin took her hand in his hands. Watching into her eyes and said "No need to fear for anything... The killer won't touch you... 'You are special to him... I mean 'me'". He hesitated and corrected.

All wondered the way Kevin spoke... Jack was to say something... but there was a knock on the door. Roberts came in.

"Hi Guys... Have I disturbed you?", Roberts said.

"No... not at all uncle...", Sherlocks said.

"Can I tell you one thing?, The killer is with us in compartment no.2", Roberts said.

Jack and Sherlocks turned to Kevin. Roberts said.

Jack and Sherlocks turned to Kevin. Roberts again said "But he is not Kevin...". Jack and Sherlocks watched their faces each other.

"Then how can you say this?", Jack asked him.

"It is a suspense... In the next stop, I will explain you." Roberts said.

Sherlocks was silent. He had a doubt on Kevin... He was unable to express it.

"Next we are going to stay in a wonderful and amazing palace of 'King Rhodes – II'. It is called 'haunted house' now-a-days". Roberts said enthusiastically.

The others didn't show any expression.

"O.K... Good night buddies", saying that Roberts left. Jack and Sherlocks despached to their cabins. The train was moving slowly taking them to the next destination.

CHAPTER VIII

THE HAUNTED HOUSE

The creeking sound of the wheels made some passengers woke up... It was night time.

Isabella watched the time... Night 1 A.M... "What happened...". The compartment was silent... Isabella switched on the light... All were sleeping... Kevin next to her bed was snoring... She came out of the cabin and was walking to take a fresh air... There was a dim lighting... Suddenly she felt that someone was moving her back... She stopped there... Her heart beat increased... Her hands were trembling... Slowly she turned her head back... No one was there. With a jerk, the train started. There was a chilly wind. She opened bath room door. Suddenly there was a chilly voice...

"How beautiful you are....", she wanted to cry but there was a knife on her throat.

"Isabella... Kevin is the luckiest one to have such a

beautiful girl friend".

"Hey… don't fear my dear. I don't want to kill you now… my way of killing is totally different… I chase you… You run and you have to request me not to kill… Wow! How beautiful the thought is!", saying that he pushed her into the luggage room and bolted it.

The banging sound of the door and cries of Isabella made everyone wakeup in the compartment No.2. Kevin ran towards the bathroom and opened it.

Everyone came there… Isabella was trembling with fear and her body was with full sweat. Tears were rolling from her eyes. Kevin took her nearer and tried to console her.

"What happened?", Roberts asked.

"When I came out of my room for fresh air, the killer attacked me…", she explained everything what happened there. There was a cut on her hand. It was a small mark with little blood stains.

The attendant came. "It is impossible sir!", the attendant remarked. No one can enter the train!"

Kevin said, "Gentleman! The killer came from another compartment".

"But sir, I am at the door sir, no one can escape from my eyes".

"This is a small compartment! No one can hide here". Jack said.

"I mean… one of the travellers in the compartment is

the killer".

All were silent they were watching the other doubt-edly. Time is 2 PM. The train is running on not caring for the incidents happened there.

"O.K... Let us move", Kevin left the place with Isabella. All went to their cabins. Kevin took her to bed.

"First ,Have a good sleep", Kevin said to her. She sighed and suddenly a thing attracted to her eyes.

"Kevin... what is it near by your bag", she sharply went there and brought it out.

'The knife with blood stains'. She wondered... turned to Kevin... Kevin face was pale... She came nearer to him with the knife.

"Kevin... what is this?"

He didn't give any reply... "Whose knife is this?"

"Isabella, really I don't know... It is not mine".

Isabella asked him, "Are you the killer?"

Keven said, "No...No..., Isabella... Don't misunderstand me". He tried to come nearer to her.

"No... Don't come near to me... I will call all", she tried to be away from him.

"O.K... O.K... I will tell you a thing now... I am not the killer, but today I am the one who attacked you... I want to play a game with you."

"What!", she surprised.

"I saw you were going out for fresh air… So, I want to play the game of the killer… just for fun…", He said.

"No… I won't believe your words", Isabella said.

"No Isabella… I swear… I will tell you all… you are my life… I have the passion to be famous as a killer… you know I read that in a paper, the psycho killer wears blue suit and eat dark chocolates… I also followed it. I like to behave like the killer. So, so many times I told you that he wouldn't kill you."

She became silent "I am tired of listening to this", she replied.

"O.K… go to sleep, Tomorrow I will explain you".

She hesitatingly came to her bed and fell on it. Thinking about all incidents, slowly she went into sleep.

Morning 6 P.M.

The train stopped before a small old building. It is a big hilly area with long pine trees. The sound of early birds chirping was a great pleasure!

The early sun rays falling on the hill make the place yellowish… The birds are already on their way for… The beautiful snow on the leaves is ready to die in the sunshine.

There is an announcement "Ladies and Gentlemen! Welcome to the palace of king Rhodes-II. Now it is called a 'haunted house'.

It is just 1 km from here. All the travellers are requested to take their luggage and follow the guards".

All the travellers followed the guards. Within 10 minutes, they reached the place that they couldn't imagine.

It is a huge building constructed with stones. It has 108 rooms. It is wonderfully architected building with gorgeous entrance. There are so many gardens, but not taken care of. They entered in a big hall with a big chandlier at the centre.

"Wow!" after entering the palace, Isabella exclaimed. "How wonderful the structure is!"

Suddenly there was an announcement. "Welcome to the palace of king Rhodes-II. The palace has been built in 1000 A.D. There is a story about king Rhodes. After constructing the palace, the king Rhodes came here with his family for hunting. But the next day, the dead bodies of the king and his family found in the hall. No one knows who killed them, but people believed that there are haunted ghosts in the Bungalow and they have killed the family of the king. People had different experiences in the bungalow".

Jack said, "Wow! It is a thrilling experience to stay here one day".

"I am the one who believe ghosts. Tonight I surely find a ghost", Roberts said.

All the travelers have been accommodated in different rooms… The authorities are taking all the precautions… guards were alert.

Kevin and Isabella have been given separate room. After entering the room, Kevin inspected it, very old room but spacious. There is a royal bed with dignity of kings and the paintings hanging on the wall showing the artistic values of those days. Every item in the room is a master piece.

"How artistically people lived in those days?" she admired.

"Ya… the room shows us how royally they spent their time". She went near by a painting. It is the painting of king Rhodes-II. She watched it closely. She found the painting watching her keenly. There was a small drizzle outside of the palace.

"How is the place!", Kevin asked him. Isabella replied, "Great… but I have the fear for…".

"For what… ghosts (or) killer".

"I don't believe ghosts… but the killer… a psycho… Tonight surely he attacks me". Kevin stared at her, "Isabella… The killer won't attack you".

Isabella surprised, "How can you say…?"

"I know it," Kevin fixedly said.

"Last night experience and your words now giving me a doubt. Are you the killer?", Isabella asked him opening her eyes wide. Kevin smiled and didn't give any reply. He came near to her and kissed on her forehead.

"I assure you… The killer won't attack you".

All the travellers are very busy with their cameras... The gardens of the palace are the centre of attraction to all.

Jack sat under the shadow of a tree... He was watching everyone silently... guards were alert and observing the people keenly.

"Hi!" Sherlocks greeted him.

"Hi", replied Jack, "I haven't imagine in my life that I can see such a nice place," Sherlocks said.

"Ya... Authorities have taken a great risk to prepare the palace like this... No one had taken care of the palace even Govt. also... but authorities of this expedition made it".

"Ya... But night time... Be careful... No one should leave the palace without protection... thick forest... haunted palace... Especially this garden... the tree which you sit under it. Jack shocked! He didn't recognise it. It is a big fearful tree with so many branches... unnoticeably he sat under it.

"Ghosts naturally attract their prey... you are feeling that unnoticeably you came here and sat, but ghosts made you come here". Roberts said.

Jack didn't believe his words. It is a big banyan tree.

Sherlocks observed the tree. He said, "There is something fishy in the tree". Suddenly rain started. They hurriedly went back to the palace. Suddenly one of the branches of the tree fell down so that someone cut the tree.

"Good evening sir", Sam wished him.

Roberts looked at the side. "Come and sit here...,"

Sam came there and sat by him.

"Coffee" Roberts asked him. Without waiting, he mixed milk with 'coffee cones'. Sam sipped it. It is very tasty!

"You are a talented man sir". Sam appreciated him. Roberts smiled but didn't give any reply to him.

"Sam, who is the next target, in your opinion?", Roberts asked.

He didn't give any reply. He questioned," sir, do you have any doubt on me?"

Roberts said, "No Sam, I don't have any doubt on you".

"Then, Sam asked him," Why don't you share any matter with me?".

Roberts laughed at him again, "Sam, you know, I have professional ethics. O.K. I strongly believe that the killer is going to attack Isabella. So, I appointed two guards for protection".

"Where?", Sam asked.

"The guards were placed before her room so that no one can enter".

"How can you guess it sir?," Sam asked.

"Generally psycho killers focus mostly on couples.

They don't have 'kick' on killing bachelors".

"Human psychology," Sam said.

"No, psycho killer psychology," Roberts said.

"Sir, if I am the killer, you have shared your views with me," Sam asked him. Roberts looked at him keenly and said, "Mr. Sam, I haven't shared everything with you. When the time comes, I will tell you".

"Can we find killer today?", Sam asked him.

"May be… or Mayn't be".

"Excuse me Sir," Roberts turned to the side. "Sir, there is someone calling you", The waiter said. He looked at the side. There is a woman of 25 years age. She is fairly typical in appearance with a long face, unexpected sloping chin, thin lips, small mouth, long nose. She dressed in business suit, but in sneekers and with back packs, She wore high heels. She looks very pretty. Roberts went near to her.

"Sorry to disturb you sir. By the way, I am saliva. Please be seated," she said.

"I am Roberts, chief security officer".

"I know sir, that's why I have called you".

"Yes madam, tell me," Roberts asked her.

"Sir, I would like to share with you a strange incident".

"What is it?", Roberts enthusiastically forwarded.

"Last night, in the train at 1 P.M, some one tried to attack me when I went to bath room", she said.

"Then why didn't you complain about it this morning?"

She didn't give any reply.

"O.K. Madam, Have you seen him?".

"Ya…He wore black suit and there is a mask on his face. Nearly 6 feet tall and he is a muscled man".

"Did he talk with you?"

"Yes, he was".

"What did he say?"

"He told me that I would be nice for him as his girl friend", she said.

Roberts was silent. He asked her, "Do you have any boy friend?".

"No sir… I am single…" she said.

"Do you have any clue about him?" He asked her.

"Yes, I have. In the attack, I found a dark chocolate wrapper in his pocket". She handed over it to him.

"Did you take it from his pocket?" Roberts took it and checked it. He easily found that 'Kevin uses the same chocolates'.

"Yes", she replied.

"Did he try to kill him?"

"Firstly, I thought that he would kill me, but he didn't attack me", she told him.

Waiter came there.

"Two coffee", she ordered.

"Madam, what do you do?"

"I work in "Hollywood studios", she said.

Roberts looked at her interestingly.

"As a make up artist", she said, "I worked for so many films with 'Canov', A famous make up man in Hollywood".

The waiter brought the coffee.

"O.K. Madam, I will look into the matter. Don't worry about it", saying that, he stood.

"Thank you sir", she said.

"You are welcome Madam", Roberts left the place.

Sam was there on his seat. He looked at the lady. But, she didn't watch him. He silently left the place.

Time 9 P.M.

King Rhodes Palace... Kevin room...

"Isabella, Are you ready?" Kevin called her.

She came out. She wore a red traditional dress consisting of a skirt with an attached bodice. It consists of a top piece that covers the torso and hangs down over the legs. The dress has sleeves, and it is held up with elastic around the chest, leaving the shoulders bare. The hem line of the dress is reaching to below the knees. The dress is made snug by featuring slits on the side of the dress that is pulled tight inorder to fit woman's figure.

She came before him and stood there like royal princess.

"Wow! Where did you get this dress?"

"I don't know… one of the authorities sent it to me".

"Who is it?"

"I don't know… I thought it would be the custom to wear this kind of dress".

"Hmm… whatever it may be… You look gorgeous in the dress." Kevin bent on his knees before her. Isabella forgot her fear and gave her right hand to him. He kissed on her hand gently. He also wore a well tailored blue suit. It would be a bit casual for the situation. Well polished black shoes, a black tie, added a great look for him.

All the guests gathered in the ball room. It has a marble flooring. There is a large space for dancing. The beautiful melodious music played by orchestra, the mesmorising lighting, dancing of couples for the music made the environment admirable.

Kevin and Isabella joined the couple. Kevin placed his right hand around her waist and left hand on her shoulder. The legs were moving rythemically along with music. She looked into his eyes. He smiled at her. Sophisticated simple movements swaying side to side are romantic. They are staying close proximity. The touch of him made her romantic. The different coloured lighting changed the mood of couples. The breathe of Isabella touched the neck of Kevin. Kevin whispered in her ears "To night is very special in my life". Isabella cheeks blushed in red colour.

The music stopped. They settled in a seat. "Wine", asking her he poured the famous well made wine in a glass.

"Cheers!", both started drinking. "Great wine!", sipping it, she exclaimed.

"Ya... specially made wine for this occasion".

"I like the hospitality of the operators".

"Ya... I also", Kevin agreed with her.

Night 11 P.M.

All the guests completed their dinner and departed to their rooms. Isabella was the special attraction to the party. Her white charming face with the gorgeous dress doubled her beauty. Isabella took the hand of Kevin and ran dragging him. Kevin was running with her. They were laughing. Suddenly she stopped him and kissed his lips. Before she could with draw, his arms were around her. His insistent mouth was parting her shaking lips, sending wild tremors along her nerves, evoking from her sensations. She had never known she was capable of feeling. He was feeling that he was just like in heaven.

They entered a passage which lead to their room. It is long and shadowy. The passage was chilly and the candles were dim on the way... They came there where foot steps are very narrow... Isabella was running leaving his hand... She was laughing...

"Isabella", Kevin warned her. "Be careful!".

Isabella, forgetting her past experiences, was running calling Kevin, "Chase me... Chase me". There were so many such passages in the palace. The moon light fell on the passage faintly making the environment different.

"Kevin... Chase me... Catch me", in the sedation of the drink, she was grumbling, murmuring... walking on the way.

"I am chasing you...", she heard a voice... Her body shivered.

"I am chasing you my dear baby", the husky voice made her sweat.

"Kevin...", she cried loudly. The passage echoed with her voice. But there was no response... The laughing sound is very nearer to her.

"Baby.. no one comes here", the shadow was closing nearer to her.

"No...No... leave me... No... I don't want to die... help me... help me..., the cries of her resounded the palace. The laugh of the shadow was bigger...

"I don't want to die... don't kill me... I don't want to

die", saying that Isabella fainted.

"Isabella… Isabella",

She opened her eyes… There was Kevin.

"Kevin… Kevin", she hugged him passionately. Tears were rolling down from her eyes… "Kevin… I don't want to die… There are ghosts in the palace… I saw one of them… I saw a shadow here".

"Why have you left me so fast?", Kevin said.

"You know the instructions… how dangerous the place it is".

"Kevin… I saw a shadow of a ghost… it chased me".

"Oh… come on Isabella… This place is a conspicuous one. May be you have watched the shadow of a statue".

"No Kevin… with my own ears I have heard its loud laughing".

A lot of guests gathered there and they were discussing.

"Is it?… OK… then the authorities will take care of it".

"O.K. all the guests move to your rooms", Roberts asked them. After listening to the cries of Isabella, they came there.

All the guests cleared the place… but Jack was silently watching the scene. Sam looked at him.

"Gentle man… can you leave this place?"

"Oh… sure", Jack left the place.

Kevin opened the room… two guards were kept for the

protection of them... Isabella directly went to bed and fell on it.

"Mood is spoiled", murmured Kevin. He went into bathroom and washed his face. The ambience was silent. Suddenly candles blew out and became dark.

Kevin didn't notice it and he stepped out of the bathroom. On the table, he found candles dim lighting doesn't cover the whole room... the curtains of the windows were moving. He was ready to blow out the candles. Suddenly there was a knock on the door. He found something strange on the knocking. The rhythemic knocking of the door made him think about it. He slowly reached the door. The silent ambience made him shiver. Suddenly he opened the door and watched the passage. There was a guard outside sitting and asked him.

"What happened sir! Any problem".

"No! No Problem..., Did anyone knock the door?"

"No sir! No one is there", the guards replied.

Kevin had a fear in his eyes. He was thinking of 'the haunted ghosts'. He closed the door and saw Isabella was in deep sleep. He sighed and watched the candles. The lighting of the candles became strange. He saw the lighting was rhythemically dancing. He didn't believe it. Suddenly a painting fell down on the floor. It made him fearful.

"Who is there?" He questioned with a voice. He saw a shadow was moving from one end to the other... His throat dried... He stood there and took a candle in his hand and went to a corner of the room where the shadow started. He found there was a door. He saw Isabella sleeping. It was an old Iron door with beautiful designs painted on it.

"How strange the room is!" He tried to open the door but it was very heavy to open it. With much difficulty he opened the door...with creeking sound the door opened. He found steps to go upstairs... The way was dirty.

"The Hidden Way...?" he wondered.

He took a candle in one hand and he started going upstairs. It was a dark narrow path and the candle light can't pierce the total darkness... The dead silence made his heart beat increased... he could hear the heart beat clearly... The steps ended to a door with blue baize. He slowly opened the door.

"Wow!" it was a beautiful room with a great furniture. In the candle light, he caught on a glimpse of himself in the queer old mirror in the room. Suddenly he found a shadow sweeping up after him. He shivered. There was a rustling noise. He turned back, but there was none. He went into the middle of the room. There were candles in the sockets of the scones. He lit them. A waiting stillness was everywhere. He advanced further and moved candle from side to side to clearly see the ambience in which he stood, suddenly he heard the foot steps of some one forwarding towards the room.

"Isabella!" His voice resounded. Footsteps suddenly

stopped.

He felt someone moving at the door. His heart beat rose… He saw a white shadow moving at the door.

"Who is there…?" he cried. The shadow came before him.

He surprised. "You! oh… No!… It is impossible".

"It is possible my dear Kevin… I am here".

He didn't get a word…

"I am a member of haunted house now… I am the shadow of yours… You know… I loved you… I begged you to love me in return… but you denied".

The white shadow suddenly disappeared. Kevin shocked at watching the shadow… The room was covered with dusty blue hangings and dark gigantic furniture.

The candles were unable to cover the vastness of the chamber. Its rays failed to pierce the end of the room. Suddenly the candles lights putout. There was darkness. Kevin tries to run. A sharp knife touched the throat of Kevin… blood spilled out like a fountain… His eyes opened with horror. The killer didn't talk much. The blood spilled on the dusty carpet of old times.

"I haven't liked the way you behaved with me… I am your favourite but today

"I AM YOUR KILLER".

Morning 6 A.M.

Isabella opened her eyes.. She had a bad headache because of hang-over... slowly. She sat on the bed turning her head... Her eyes searched for Kevin... The chilly wind touched her body when she removed window curtains... The Sun rays in the chilly wind gave pleasure to her body... She can't hear of any sound there... suddenly she found a strange thing on the floor. She took it and found that a small sharp weapon engraved on it."I AM YOUR KILLER"

... she cried in horror "Kevin!". She can't get reply... In the corner, she found the door open... Her heart beat rose and ran towards the door in panic. She went upstairs through the steps. Her loud cry resounded the total palace.

"It is the work of ghosts", some one commented.

After hearing the cries of Isabella, guards alerted and went in.

They found the dead body of Kevin and fainted Isabella .They hurriedly informed Roberts, the chief security officer. Roberts came there with Sam. The news of Kevin's death spread like a wild fire .

" It is the work of the killer, look at his forehead. It is engraved 'I AM YOUR KILLER" Another one commented.

"No... The haunting ghosts surely attacked him last night", A woman in horror commented.

"May be Isabella killed him, because no one can enter the room", another woman commented.

"Sam... Do you believe that it is the work of the killer?" Roberts said.

"Yes sir... simple reason is the symbolic writing 'I AM YOUR KILLER'", He gave reply to Roberts.

Roberts said, "Sam, I guess it is not the work of the killer".

Sam surprised, "What!"

"Yes, I feel that some one who knows the way of psycho killer killing attacked Kevin and killed".

"How can you know sir?", Sam asked him.

"Because of this...", he showed a ring in the blood shed.

"Whose ring is this", Sam asked him curiously.

"Let me check it", he put the ring in the plastic cover and sealed it.

"May be the ring is the psycho killer's".

Roberts didn't give any reply... guards didn't allow people come near to the death spot.

After coming out of the room, they were moving to office. Suddenly there was a rough voice.

"Excuse me Gentlemen!"

"Yes", Roberts replied.

"Last night at 2 PM, I saw a stranger going on outside of the palace... I have night vision Binoculars. Using them,

I found that he went on to the train side".

"Is it?... O.K." Roberts said, "Thank you Gentleman! We will consider your words, we investigate in the way".

"Sam", Roberts said. "Shall we go back to the train?", He said.

"Sure", Sam replied.

They both went out of the palace to investigate.

Roberts and Sam both reached the train. There was none... Roberts came to compartment No. 2. He opened the door and entered. He sat by the window... Sam sat opposite to him.

"Sam...I also travelled in the same compartment... But the killer didn't target me upto this time... It is strange to tell that the killer targeted only couples.

"No sir... first the killer targeted Elisa".

"Ya... Elisa... Do you know she was a strange girl. One-day she suspiciously behaved. She was talking hysterically herself. Although I called her, she didn't take care of my words..." Roberts said.

"Poor girl..." Sam showed sympathy on Elisa.

"Sam... why Kevin was killed?" Roberts questioned.

"I don't have any idea sir... first I thought the killer killed him... but now may be in the name of killer, someone killed him".

"What about Isabella?" Roberts asked him suddenly.

"May be she is the killer of Kevin because no one can

enter the room", Sam replied.

"Gather information about Isabella and her background", Roberts requested him.

"Sure sir", Sam replied.

Suddenly they found someone was moving at the compartment door. Roberts silently signaled Sam to continue his talking.

"Sir... I have a doubt on Jack also".

"Hmm..", saying that Roberts slowly went to the door and opened. There was a train guard standing outside.

"Good Morning Sir, I am 'Archard', the train guard here". He replied without listening to question.

Roberts moved his head "Gentleman! Have you seen any stranger here in the area?"

"No sir... last night I slept here in my guard room locking the door. I dind't find anything strange."

"Don't you have fear?", Sam asked him.

"No sir! I am habituated to it".

"Can I visit your cabin once?", Roberts asked.

"Sure sir... come on... He took them to the last compartment i.e., guards room".

"He opened the door of it. It is not the ordinary guard room like the other trains have... It has been specially designed for the travel... A small bed with all the facilities...

Entering the cabin, Roberts eyes observed all the things keenly.

"A small place with good comforts', the guard said.

"Ya... the great place to stay in", Roberts said.

"O.K... Gentle man; we have to leave now", saying that Roberts signalled Sam.

Both came out, "Good day sirs", guard saluted them.

"Great day man", Roberts replied.

CHAPTER IX

THE SERIOUS SEARCHING

All the guests packed their bags and were ready to come back to the train. The serial deaths of co-passengers grieved them a lot. All were discussing about the travellers of compartment No.2. "Isabella... don't cry", Jack sat near by her. Isabella was silent and tears were rolling down from her cheeks.

"This is horrible!", Sherlocks terrified after listening to the news of the death of Kevin, he became very dull. He pleaded the authorities to shift his place from compartment no.2 to other compartment. But they assured him to provide tight security in the compartment.

Authorities made a decision to conclude the tour one day earlier. All the travellers relieved after listening to the decision. Most of them are willing to get back their homes.

"Sam... Did you find any strange thing in the guard's

room", Roberts asked him.

"Ya... I found two glasses half filled on the table".

"Ya... good observation... I feel something fishy about it", Roberts said.

Sam nodded his head with agreement. "Yes... may be there is another one staying in the room".

"We should enquire him to clear our doubts", they called on the guard. He came there and stood there.

"Sit down... gentlemen". He sat on a chair.

"Before we came to your compartment, any one had visited you?".

"Yes sir... locomotive operator' Mr. George visited me... we had juice".

The doubts are cleared... the three sat silently.

"Thank you Gentleman... you can go", Roberts said.

"The beauty of the journey is lost!", Sherlocks exclaimed sadly.

He was in jack cabin. The train was returning to Manchester... There was no glow in his face.

"Ya... It is the disastrous journey I have ever made", Jack said.

"Food order sir!", the attendant came there.

"I don't want to have anything".

There was a knock on the cabin door. Roberts came in and sat with them.

'Sir, can you tell me who is the killer?", Jack asked him.

"Yes… he belongs to compartment No.2. He is a split personality".

"Means sir?", Sherlocks asked him.

"The killer, with us, behaves like an ordinary gentleman, but coming to be an individual, he shows his original nature".

"Oh!", Sherlocks exclaimed.

"O.K guys! Bye", saying that Roberts directly went into the cabin of Isabella.

"May I come in?" Roberts asked.

"Please, come in sir", Isabella replied.

She sat at a corner of her seat… not interested on anything.

Roberts went nearer to her, "Isabella… sorry for asking you… Do you remember any unwanted incident happened between you and Kevin".

"No, I can't remember anything unusual happened between Kevin and I".

"Has he used any unusual words with you?"

"Ya… I remember. Two days back, he told me that the killer wouldn't kill me".

"How strange… The killer killed Kevin and not you…

that means the killer has concern on you... I guess, Kevin knew the killer", saying that, Roberts stared into the eyes of the killer. Her eyes were still. There is no feeling in them.

"Do you have any doubt on any one?", Roberts asked her.

"No! I don't have any idea", she said.

"Do you remember any sound (or) any unwanted scenes that night Kevin was killed?"

"No sir... I was in deep sleep?"

"Hmm...", sighed Roberts.

"O.K. Isabella ... Thank you", he said.

"You are welcome sir", she said. Roberts came out of the cabin. The train was moving fast. He thought that someone was observing him.

Night 1 PM...

The train was moving through the beautiful landscapes to reach its destination. Isabella was in her cabin alone... She didn't sleep... Suddenly she heard the foot steps of someone. She was in alert. there was a knock on the door. She didn't reply. Her heart beat rose. She sweated again there was a knock.

"Who is there?", she was shivering.

"Ma'm... guards... Roberts sent us for your protection",

there was a reply.

"Then why are you knocking the door?", she asked him.

"Ma'm… please open the door. We have to handover the letter given by Roberts".

Her heart beat rose fast… She didn't give any reply… the dim light of night bulb dipped three times… She was in terror… She wanted to make a loud cry… but with fear she can't open her mouth… her lips are shivering… There was a bang on the door… She didn't give any reply… the sound of moving train is now horrible to her ears… Suddenly the knocks stopped. There was utter silence. She sat at the corner of the seat.

Suddenly she found a smoke in the compartment… Something bad smell… She found that they weren't guards… She wanted to cover her nose with a mask… But the smoke was very thick… Her eyes were blistering… She was in utter shock… She opened her mouth to cry… but smoke went into her throat… She was unable to move… she thought it would be better come out of cabin and face the situation.

She opened the door… The chilly wind gushed on her face… No one was there… there was a confusion.

"Isabella… at last you came out like a rat coming out from its hole", the voice of the killer shook her. She tried to run but the knife of the killer stopped her.

"Don't move my baby… otherwise you will be killed?", showing the sharp tip of the knife to her.

"Who are you and why are you attacking all like

this?", she asked. The killer didn't give reply. He asked her again a question "Isabella...tell me... 'WHY YOU KILLED KEVIN?".

Isabella was silent. Her face was pale. He brought out a rope and silently tied her hands and legs of Isabella.

She was in utter shock and didn't know what to do. He has a knife which has a bend at the end...

"Isabella... you are a clever girl... I know why you killed Kevin in the name of mine...", the killer said. "You were a cheater... you with your boyfriend Sherlocks planned to trap Kevin... Kevin had given you a million dollars as a debt... He didn't take any surity from you... He believed you... because you are his fiancy... but you don't like to marry him... you are a great lover of Sherlocks... To remove Kevin from your path, this was the best time... poor Kevin... He thought that you would marry him... He really doesn't know how cruel you are... How cruelly you killed him", he stopped.

"Actually I don't want to kill you... But you made me to kill you".

The killer put knife on her throat, "I don't like your attitude... You killed him... blame is on me... no, it's not the way you should behave." saying that, the killer was ready to cut her throat.

"Stop there!", the rough voice of Roberts alerted the killer. Roberts came out from a shadow. In his hand, there is a revolver.

"I know... you will surely come for Isabella... I know".

Roberts said, "I don't know why you are killing the people in compartment No.2".

Saying that, Roberts was ready to remove the mask of the killer.

"No... don't come near... I will kill Isabella", the killer said.

Roberts stopped. Isabella was in horror... She doesn't know what to do... the sharp knife on her throat brought chill on her body... The train is moving fast... The darkness of the forest, the chilly wind from windows makes them worried.

"Leave her man...", Roberts warned him.

"Ssh...", the knife cut the throat of Isabella and the killer jumped out of the moving train.

"No...", said Roberts, but it was of no use... He didn't expect the quick reaction of the killer...

The throat was bleeding. Roberts pulled the red chain. The train stopped. Doctors were called... they tested Isabella. They took her into medical emergency room in the train... While doctors were taking her to the room... she made a sign to Roberts to come near to her.

She wrote in his hand with blood 'E', Roberts looked at the letter intently...

"Is there any hope sir?", Sam asked Roberts.

"Doctors said... no hope...", taking the cigar out from his pocket and tried for lighter. Sam took lighter and lit it...

"Thank you...", Roberts said puffing the cigar.

"How do you know Isabella would be attacked".

"Because Isabella killed Kevin and put blame on the killer", Roberts said slowly.

Sam wondered... Isabella thought that she would easily escape, but her plans didn't work out.

"Can I get a cup of coffee now", Roberts asked.

"Sure sir...", taking the intercom, Sam ordered coffee.

Sipping the coffee, Roberts asked, "Sam, can I ask you something?".

"Sure sir".

"Why are you helping the killer?" Roberts asked him calmly.

Sam shivered...His hands were trembling... "What are you talking sir?", he said.

Roberts took out the revolver from his pocket... pointed it to Sam... "Why Sam... why are you helping him.. Who is the killer, tell me".

"O.K sir... I will tell you... down the gun", he said.

Roberts downed the gun. But suddenly Sam took out his revolver, kept it on his fore head and shot on his head himself... Roberts didn't expect it. The bullet came out of his head making a hole.

Austin's chamber...

"What is going on Gentleman, I don't understand", Austin asked Roberts.

Sam's death was a sensation... Austin called on to the chairman's chamber on train.

"Sir, Sam is the secret helper to the killer", he helped the killer at different places and caused for the death of passengers.

"Why... why he has done like that?".

"Sir, I don't know... but I have some idea about the killer. I am going to catch him".

"Mr. Roberts, I believe you. But my wish is you have to catch the killer at the earliest".

"Sir, I will do my level best...", saying that, Roberts came out of Austin's chamber.

"Isabella... open your eyes", Roberts called her. She recovered some what. Doctors told him that she couldn't move and speak now.

"Is she out of danger doctor?", he asked.

"No... It takes at least 12 hours. Then only we can tell you about her condition". He came out and directly went into the dining car. There were some passengers dining there. He went into a corner and occupied a seat.

"What do you want for?", waiter asked him.

"A cup of black coffee…"

"Snacks sir?",

"No… thank you".

"You are welcome sir", he took his cigar out but put it in his pocket because it is no smoking zone. Waiter brought coffee. The smell of fresh beans give him life.

"Great coffee…", sipping it he admired it. Suddenly he saw a woman was watching him, he greeted her. She also greeted him in return.

"Excuse me", he asked her "Where are you from?".

"I am Chelsia from London. Nice to meet you."

"Nice to meet you too".

"Can I tell you something?"

"Sure"

"Tonight, the killer is going to attack you".

Chelsia shocked. She stared at him.

"Ya… I have got information… you are going to be attacked".

"What can I do sir?" she asked him.

"Please, come with me".

She followed him. Roberts took her to his office. "Please be seated". She sat a chair.

"Yes sir, tell me. Why the killer attacks me?" Roberts watched her silently.

"Madam, I think you are from London, right?"

"Ya sir", she replied.

"Madam… If you answer to my questions correctly… I free you."

"What… what is going on here. I don't know".

"Madam… you know everything… Tell me… Why have you sheltered the killer at home?"

Chelsea wondered… "What do you mean? What are you talking to?"

"Don't pretend… I know everything".

"Officer… You are mistaken. I haven't given shelter to any one".

"Madam, tell me… This cc camera footages tells you".

"He opened his computer and showed her that a person who has worn a black suit and a mask on face entering her house in 'vintage apartment' in black bourn street, London.

"Our investigating officers in London traced the footage and sent the information to me that you allowed the stranger into your apartment.

Chelsea didn't give any reply. Her face was dull.

"Chelsea… you can't escape from here… tell me, who is the killer? Why are you helping her?"

Suddenly Chelsea brought out a knife from her pocket and attacked Roberts.

Roberts was alert. He escaped from her attack... But suddenly there is an unwanted incident... Chelsea cut her throat herself... Her throat was bleeding.

"Oh shit!" said Roberts. He shifted her to the medical car, but it was of no use. Roberts was called on to Austin's office.

"Mr. Roberts... What are these things?"

"Sir... Chelsea is the helper of the killer... I found her and questioned her. She suddenly committed suicide. I didn't expect it".

Austin was silent. He didn't want to give any suggestion to Roberts.

"In the next hour, I am going to catch the killer".

The words made Austin silent.

CHAPTER X

THE KILLER REVEALED!

The train was running to reach its destination. All the passengers want to return their homes at the earliest. The horrible incidents happened in the journey made them fearful.
"A horrible tour it is!" A traveller exclaimed.

"Ya…" said another.

It is the place where all the smokers can gather in the train. Roberts was watching everyone silent.

"Hi Roberts, this is mongrel".

He turned his head. There was a woman whose age is barely 22 standing there.

"Yes Madam… How do you know my name?"

"I saw you in the haunted house…".

"Ya… great. How may I help you?"

"Ya...sir...I want to tell you an incident happened recently in my compartment".

"What happened?"

"Sir, a woman named Chelsea came to me and introduced a girl".

"In the train?"

"Yes, she introduced me that she was her friend and she was also very much interested in adventures".

"So..."

Then they both offered me a drink coming to my cabin and after that I fell asleep".

Roberts was listening her words interestingly "One woman in that is 'Chelsea".

"Excuse me", asking that Roberts lit his cigar.

"A woman was with her... 'Ha', I don't remember..." Her name starts with I think 'S'?

"Next what happened".

"I fell asleep nearly 3 hours".

"Why did they do like that. Did they steal anything from your cabin?"

"No sir, but they used my cabin for a purpose".

"Did you find anything strange in your cabin?"

"Yes sir, If you come with me, I will show you". He went with her upto her compartment.

"Please, come in sir", opening her cabin, he entered the cabin.

"This cabin is for two members. You are alone staying it?"

"Ya sir... I reserved it for me only".

"Is it possible?"

"Yes... double payment" she said to him.

He inspected the cabin... It was a big cabin with two beds having luxurious facilities.

"Anyone knows about it".

"Ya... Chelsea... She knows it that I am alone in the cabin. She misused it. She became my friend in the train. I trusted her".

"So she took advantage of it", he proclaimed these thing I found when Chelsea left the place.

There was a face mask wearing full, torch light and bands with 'E' tags and bangles.

"Did you wear the face mask?"

"No sir"

"O.K... I will wear... What result should I get, I want to know".

He wore the face mask and stood before the mirror.

He was shocked to find...

It is the face mask of the Railway guard, Archard.

"When did they come to your cabin?" "before we went to haunted house".

"When did you find this mask in this cabin?"

"This morning I found these things in the box which is kept under my bed".

"Where is the box?"

"Here sir...", she dragged a box out from her bed.

"Oh my God!" Roberts exclaimed.

The box was very familiar to him.

"I saw the same box in compartment No.2", he said.

Mongrel shocked.

"What!"

"Yes"

"Whose box is it sir?"

"Can you identify that woman when you see her".

"Yes... I can draw her picture also".

"Oh... great... Are you an artist?"

"Yes... I am a born artist", taking a white sheet and fixing it to the board, she said.

Roberts was watching her interestingly. She took out pencils from her box and started drawing her face...It has taken ten minutes time to draw... Her fingers are moving artistically. Finally she has drawn...

"Here she is sir!", she showed him the picture.

It is a picture of a girl aged 22 (or) 23. Her eyes are thin. She has small eyes having no smile on it. Her curved lips and curly hair made him think that he has seen her somewhere.

"I saw her", Roberts tried to remember the girl.

"Yes...", he remembered.

She was nearly 'Saliva', whom he met her in the haunted house dining room.

"Can you come with me", Roberts asked her.

"Sure sir!" she replied.

Roberts informed Austin that the killer was there in the train. Roberts took two guards and went to compartment No.4 and asked a man about her sharing the picture.

"Yes... She is 'Saliva'... she stays in compartment No.4, cabin No.2".

"Is she in the cabin now?" he questioned.

"Ya... mostly she doesn't come out of the cabin".

Roberts with guards went to the compartment and directly he went to cabin no.4.

He asked the guards to be silent. All the other passengers were watching the scene silently.

He knocked the door silently. He didn't get any reply. The cabin was locked inside.

"Madam", Roberts called her.

Roberts didn't get any reply. He waited 3 minutes. He signed the guards to break the door.

Suddenly the door opened. It was 'Saliva'… She was the same as in the drawn picture.

"Hello officer…", she greeted him.

"Hello Madam", he replied.

"What a sudden surprise! Come in…", she asked him.

He entered the cabin. There was no one in the cabin.

"Are you alone in the cabin!" he asked her.

"No… I have another one with me, Chelsia", she said.

She was very cool and calm.

"Can I ask you a question?"

"Sure sir" she said.

"Is this mask made by you?" showing the mask of train guard, he asked.

"Ya sir… Train guard asked me to make".

"Oh! I see… can I see your art?"

"Sure sir…", she opened her box and brought out so many tools. He interestingly watched them.

"O.K. Madam…. See you soon".

"You are always welcome".

Chairman's chamber…

Austin was writing a letter. He wasn't in good mood. There was a knock on the door.

"Yes... come in".

Roberts entered the room. He greeted Austin.

"Come in Roberts... Have a seat?", Roberts seated.

"Coffee?", Austin asked.

"Yes".

Austin rang the bell... attendant entered.

"Coffee".

"Yes sir...", Attendant went out.

"Sir, I have got an idea... Who is the killer?"

"Then why are you waiting for", Austin asked.

"With proofs, I would like to catch her".

"Her?...A lady is doing all this".

"I am sure... she is the killer"

"How can you prove it?"

Roberts showed him a file. It has nearly 100 papers. The door was knocked.

"Come in...", Austin said.

The attendant came in with a beautiful smelly auromatic coffee.

"Thank you", Roberts said to attendant.

"You are welcome sir", saying that he went out.

"So... finally we are going to catch the killer".

"Yes sir".

"Roberts... Do you know within a day, we are going to end our journey".

"I know sir... This time I won't disappoint you... I take leave on".

"O.K. Roberts", Roberts replied.

Roberts directly went to the Train Driver's cabin.

"Hi sir!"The Train guard greeted him.

"Hi!How are you?"

"Fine sir,Thanks for visiting my compartment first time."

"First time!", Roberts confused"Sir,You forgot me I think".

"No sir,I saw you in the haunted house ,All knew you are a detective from England", The Train guard said.

"But on the day,I met you in the same compartment".

"On which day",

"That day when Kevin was killed".

"Sorry sir,You are mistaken,At that time I was in the 'HAUNTED HOUSE',not in the compartment.I didn't meet you".

Roberts confused."No sir,I came to your cabin and you only invited Sam and me".

"No sir,I was there in the haunted house…You are mistaken."

"Oh my God… then", He ran hurriedly back to compartment No.4.

"So, saliva acted as a train guard…", he concluded that the killer is 'Saliva'. But there is a confusion for him. He asked two security guards to come with him. Directly he went up to her cabin. His heart beat rose.

He knocked the door. The door was open. There was no saliva in the compartment. All the passengers were watching them curiously.

"Come on boys… quick!" He enquired the other passengers.

"Did you see Saliva!", He enquired the other passengers.

"Sir, I have seen the train guard coming out from her cabin", one of the passengers gave information about it.

"Who…?" he wondered.

"Train guard… 2 minutes back".

"Impossible… I saw him in his compartment now!"

He got idea, "Oh my God! Hurry up!" with guards he ran to the last compartment. The two guards followed him.

They reached there. The door was closed. There was silence. Roberts knocked the door. Guards were ready with their guns. Roberts was alert. There was the sound of opening the door. Guards were alert. The train guard stood there.

"Yes sir… What happened!", he asked.

"Stop there… Raise your hand", Roberts shouted. He raised his hands. Roberts entered the room. There was something unusual. There was a sound coming from bathroom.

"Who is there?", Roberts asked him.

There was no reply. He tried to go near of bathroom. Suddenly the train guard jumped out of the train. All were shocked.

"Stop the train! Pull the chain!", saying that Roberts ran. A Guard pulled the chain. The train stopped with creeking sound. The guard was running. There was something unusual in his running. Roberts chased him. The two guards followed him.

"Stop there…", saying that Roberts shot him. The bullets pierced his legs. He screamed with pain. He tried to run but he was unable to run. His legs were bleeding. Roberts reached him. Suddenly he took a knife from his pocket and tried to cut his throat. Roberts cleverly stopped it by hitting on his hand.

'No', saying that, he tried to escape. But Roberts and two guards caught him. He was unable to stand because he was wounded and blood was streaming out of his two legs.

He was surrounded by security guards. Austin came there… He was fully wounded. Security guards tied his hands and he was taken to a compartment.

"Roberts, is he the killer?", Austin asked.

"Sir, come with me", saying that Roberts went hurriedly into the compartment of train guard. Directly he went into the bath room. Austin followed him.

There was a shock!

There was the train guard with wounds. His legs and hands were tied.

"Oh, my God!", Roberts wondered. Two train guards with same features!

"Then whom had we caught!", he exclaimed. Roberts went near to him. He was wounded. He was moaning. The security guards released him.

"Come guards... quick", saying that he went to the caught one.

"Who are you?", he asked him.

He didn't give any reply.

"Remove your face mask", Roberts ordered him. All are watching him curiously. There was tight security. They were eager to know who is the killer.

Roberts went near to him. The killer's eyes were sharp. He was trying to escape. But it was of no use. Roberts came forward, two guards hold him tightly. Roberts removed his face mask. All were shocked and wondered.

It was not 'He'! It was 'She'!

'IT WAS ELISA'.

All the people didn't believe, Roberts was in shock.

Austin didn't believe. It was a shock for everyone. All thought she was the one who was killed first! But not... Tears were rolling out from the eyes of 'Elisa'.

Roberts sat near to her and asked her "Are you the serial killer?"

She nodded her head "Yes, I am".

"I am the serial killer... I am the one who killed three members in London".

Roberts, Austin and everyone was silent. They didn't have words to speak. How cleverly she played the game.

"What about Saliva?" Austin questioned her. She didn't give any reply.

"Madam, please confess the mistakes you have done. Then only you can get a relaxation in punishment". But she didn't give any reply. Roberts made a sign to all to leave the compartment. He kept with him two guards.

Austin and all the people who gathered there left the place. Austin removed her ties. Again the train resumed its journey. Roberts lit the cigar.

"Cigarette", he offered her.

"No," she said, "I need some water".

Roberts asked a guard to get water for her.. A guard went out to get water. Roberts sat before her. He asked her.

"Elisa! I didn't believe it. Why you became like this".

"When I was a kid, my mother was divorced. She didn't have any money with her. She begged on the roads. I saw with my own eyes how people behaved with her. Some took advantage of her poverty. Before my own eyes, people bullied my mother, sometimes beat her . I didn't get food sometimes. It made me depressed. I hated the society, the people especially men. But my mother struggled for me and joined me in good schools. Because of my mother's poverty and inability, people bullied me also. I have suffered a lot in the hands of society. When I came to 16, my neighbor tried to rape me. Although my mother obstructed him, he kicked her and raped me. It was unbearable for me. That day onwards, I wanted to take revenge on the society.

I decided to kill the people. But for so many years I didn't dare to do it. I read so many books. In the education, I was a topper. I got a job also. But, the incidents happened in my life haven't stopped me doing all these things.

Whenever I saw a couple, I remember my childhood days. I don't have any repent on my behavior. Whatever the punishment I get, I am ready to face all the consequences".

"What abot Saliva"Roberts repeated.

"I killed her and make her worn mask of mine .All thought i died .I was in the place of Saliva and my friend chelsia helped me in it".

Roberts was silent. The guards arrested her.

Police Head Quarters

London, 11 A.M.

All the officials were very busy. The news of the serial killer spread like a wild fire. The chief of the police is going to conduct a meeting at 11 A.M. All the press personnel are coming to the hall. The conference hall was very busy. The chief with Roberts came to the hall at 11 AM.

The chief started the meeting. "Ladies and gentleman... It is sad to announce that the killer killed 13 people brutally. The serial killer name is 'Elisa'." She was brought before the press personnel. Her face was covered with cloth mask. The remaining details will be given by our chief investigative officer, Roberts.

"Thank you sir," Roberts spoke, "Ladies and Gentlemen, As you know that the serial killings of innocent people frightened every one. At last, we found the real culprit 'Elisa'. Elisa graduated from London school of Economics. She is a brilliant student in the college. She received bitterest experiences in her life. When she was doing her graduation, she loved Kevin, but unfortunately she was rejected by him. She was in depression and she didn't know how to overcome her depression. She had the habit of visiting theatres and beaches. She liked the play 'As I know how to kill'. Because the characters in the play are very similar to her life.

Everyday she went to the theatre and watched the play because she got satisfaction. When the murder scene arrives, she stands and makes loud shouts. In her depression, she killed a police officer and she felt that it was a thrilling experience for her. After that, she went to a beach and saw a couple.

She thought that if she would kill them. She would became a sensation. She had the habit of making masks. She prepared the masks very easily. After killing the couples in the beach, all the people discussed about the killer. She watched fear in their eyes. She felt thrilled.

She travelled in the coverly hills train and created the impression that she had been killed by the psycho killer. But no one knows that she has killed 'Saliva' and she entered the train in her place wearing Saliva face mask. After that, she started killing the passengers in compartment No.2 one by one.

"Why she had killed the people in compartment No.2", one of the journalists questioned.

"Killers don't have any reasons. She had killed all of them for her pleasure".

"Any other questions?"

"Sir, why she has chosen couples?"

"Because her father killed her mother, it made her marriage is a dangerous proposal".

"Why had she killed a police man?"

"To show her recognition. Generally psychos kill others for fame. They get satisfaction also".

"O.K. Thank you all", saying that the chief stood there. The meeting ended. All the press personnels were leaving the place. Then, the chief asked Roberts a question.

"What is the position of Isabella and Sam".

"Sam who is the helper in the act is the best friend of Elisa. He knows everything. He is recovering. He confessed everything what he did.Isabella is recovering".

"How she managed everything on the train?"

"With the help of Sam only, he is the one who helped her a lot".

The police were taking 'Elisa' to the vehicle.

"Excuse me, can I get a glass of water?" Elisa requested a police personnel who was with her.

The police man gave her a water bottle. She had water and suddenly she took the revolver from police man. He surprised at her speed and tried to prevent her to take the revolver. But it was too late. She put the revolver on her head.

"Good bye...", saying that she fired herself. The sound made everyone alert. Roberts, the chief ran to her.

But ,it was of no use. Roberts took her hand. She was lying there with open eyes and her lips were smiling saying that

"I AM NOT THE LOSER".

The End ?

EPILOGUE

Hammer Smith hospital,
London.

The dead body of 'Elisa' was taken to post mortem room.The police officers were waiting outside.The doctors come out of the postmortem room hurriedly. "Officer" He called one of the police officers.He asked him"Is it the dead body of Elisa?"."

"Yes,we have brought It from the death spot",The officer replied."come inside",The doctor asked him.The police officer entered the room and shocked.The mask of the dead body is removed."That is not Elisa!".

"Excuse me",There is a sweet voice.An old man raised his head.It was 11pm and in the small street ,There is no one."Yes,What do you want?".

"I am your killer",The young man said."What!" The oldman wondered." Bang",The hammer touched the head of the old man."I wanna kill you,I wanna kill you".

'THE KILLING STARTED AGAIN'

AFTERWORD

From my childhood days on wards,I like thriller zoners andso I decided towrite A psycho thriller .Before I started writing the book,I didn't have any idea what to write.But when I started writing,- flawlessly I have written this book.Thanks to my Lord' Shiva' for giving me this creative talent.I hope the readers enjoy my first novel"The coverly Hills", A Psycho Thriller.

ACKNOWLEDGEMENT

"I would like to thank my wife K.Padmavathi ,My daughter K.Alekhya and My son K.Munikiran who has helped me a lot to complte this book.I am very much thankful to all my friends M.Srinivasulu,Suresh,sampath,Prasad   who have helped me in creating this book."

ABOUT THE AUTHOR

Kalimisetty Anandbabu

Kalimisetty Anand babu, pen name of Kalimisetty, was born and brought up in Proddatur, Kadapa (dt), Andhra Pradesh, India. He was a familiar author in his native language, Telugu. His father was a well known singer in 'Telugu Folk Songs'.  He is basically well known English lecturer and he was a specialist in 'Writing Psycho Thriller'. His present novel 'Coverly Hills' is a psycho thriller with the sub tag of 'I am your killer' is an extra ordinary psycho thriller which gives neck to neck thrilling while reading.Although,It is his fist novel in English,his grip on writing on thriller is impeccable.

PRAISE FOR AUTHOR

"Kalimisetty Anandbabu created the original qulitative psycho thriller which gives reader thrilling experience every minute.The grip on the story made him that I think this is not the first novel for him.The creativity of the story make the reader transport intothe new world.

K.srenivasulu,A.D.E.

Genco,Andhrapradesh